Beauty's Alien Beast

By

Linda Mooney

BEAUTY'S ALIEN BEAST
Copyright © 2010 by *Linda Mooney*
Print ISBN 978-1730793653

Editor: Chelly Peeler
Cover Art: Ash Arceneaux

Chapter One
01:38 Hours

The music was too fucking loud. In fact, it was almost eardrum-shattering loud, but the crowd didn't seem to mind. As a matter of fact, on second thought, the loud music was all right with her. This way she couldn't hear those nasty little devils whispering in her head. As long as she stayed here and drank herself into mindless oblivion, she could live with herself for another day.

As she relaxed in a corner booth, Maurra casually kept an eye on the clientele coming and going from the bar. They were a rag-tag lot, mostly miscreants and questionable criminals, as the higher class customers kept their distance from places like this. This time of night there were more people coming in than heading out, which meant there was a greater chance of someone getting pissed and slitting open someone else's abdomen, or a body part that resembled an abdomen. If and when that happened, she'd have to step in and assert her authority, whether she wanted to or not.

That was another thing about being here that she liked. She could handle drunks better when she'd downed a few herself. Especially mean drunks. She could bash their skulls in with little guilt.

The music died briefly, long enough for the band to quench its six throats. The semi-quiet would be short-lived.

Creatures around her continued their chitter-chatter. Some used electronic translators. Some had implants. Most conversed as best they could with sign language and the occasional grunt, along with a smattering of Varonese, the universal language at this end of the Carbucharon galaxy.

Maurra uncrossed her ankles and re-crossed them where she was resting her feet on the seat across from her. Here in the near darkness at the far end of the room, and away from the door and stage, her deep scarlet uniform was almost black in color. It was the best camouflage she could manage. However, there were several patrons who had already spotted her. Although they didn't know her personally, the crest in the center of her chest identified her as a JoJo. For some, they moved closer, as if having her nearby ensured their safety. For others, they quickly moved to the other side of the bar, or left altogether before she could discover what nefarious nastiness they were up to.

It didn't matter. Her initial job on this planet was completed. The bad guys had been caught and were awaiting extradition. The bosses had sent her their congratulations. She figured she deserved a little rest and relaxation before boarding her own flight back to Narcissus and the station where she resided.

Sighing, she took another sip of her drink. Whatever the stuff was, it was potent. Gulping it outright could put her in the hospital in no time flat. Sipping it would not only keep her insides from blowing up, but it would also make the drink last longer. She wouldn't need more than one stein of this stuff to make her ass-over-elbows drunk, anyway.

A scuffle at the end of the bar drew her attention. Maurra squinted to clear her vision the same moment a loud and definitely irritated roar nearly shattered the nearby mugs. It was an Ellinod and what looked like two Par Mattas. She grunted. This should be good. The Ellinod was at least two meters taller, and a goodly number of kilos heavier than both

Par Mattas bolted together. She continued to watch the scene unfold, but already she could feel her body steeling itself just in case she needed to step in.

The slimy Par Mattas were squeaking up a storm and waving their tentacles in the air. They were either excited or pissed off. Or both. Maurra wondered how the Ellinod fit in. The beastly looking creatures were loners. They didn't do business with other species outside of their mining operations, and rarely ventured away from their home world. When they did, however, it had to be for a damn good reason.

A frown creased her forehead. The Ellin system was a good two dozen or more light years from here. What in the world would an Ellinod be doing on Cura-Cura in the first place?

Now her internal alarm was going off, warning her that too many variables weren't adding up properly. Slowly, almost nonchalantly, Maurra unhooked her ankles and lowered her booted feet to the floor. She sat up straighter, never taking her eyes away from the scene that was drawing more attention to itself.

The Ellinod's gnarly face was almost gray in color. From the little she knew about the creatures, that gray was a sign the monster was upset. No. He was angry.

No. Correction again. He was livid.

If he reaches out and grabs one of those —

The Ellinod threw back its head and let go with another roof-rattling roar, raising massively-muscled arms ending in fists that looked ready to pound the Par Mattas into oblivion. Suddenly, and without warning, a thick arm shot out, and the enormous hand closed around several sections of the Par Mattas, catching them both in its steely grip. Before anyone could react, the other arm reached down and scooped the semi-aquatic blobs up against its chest. Striding over to the doorway, the Ellinod heaved the two creatures out into the street amid squalling, screeching, and screaming.

For two whole seconds the patrons of the bar held their breaths, waiting to see what the enormous Ellinod would do next. When it gave its huge, curved horns a shake, and a little shrug of its enormous, muscular shoulders, then turned to resume its seat at the bar, the place gave a silent sigh of relief, and things went back to normal.

Maurra had no idea she'd gotten to her feet, one hand lightly resting on the butt of her psionic pistol, until a Madranite scuttled past her and hurried away. Cursing silently, Maurra tried to blend back into the shadows but it was too late. The Ellinod had already noticed her. Or maybe it had noticed her long before the incident started. It was hard to tell, and frankly she hadn't been trying very hard to remain incognito.

The first thing she noticed was that the creature wasn't dressed like a typical Ellinod. The usual coarse shirt and baggy pants that most of them wore was replaced with a smart-looking, high-quality dark blue shirt and vest, and black, form-fitting breeches. Instead of sandals, this one wore heavy black boots. It was also bigger than most Ellinod she had encountered in the past. Bigger and taller, and wider. There wasn't an ounce of extra fat on it, meaning this one was used to hard labor. Maurra looked back up at the thing's face to find it staring at her. The expression was brooding, almost as if it was trying to send her a silent signal.

A shiver went down her spine. Icy cold, it sent an additional warning to her brain. Her body automatically went into JoJo mode as her muscles hardened. She could already feel the familiar tingling in the middle of her forehead as her psionic powers focused.

The beast must have noticed the translucent glittering. Her power would have stood out in the shadows like a beacon. Slowly, the Ellinod shook its ponderous head with its enormous horns that stretched all the way to the ends of its shoulders, and resumed sipping its drink. But the creature continued to keep an eye on her. For what reason, she couldn't begin to guess.

It was difficult to tell whether the thing was male or female. Both sexes looked almost identical as long as their clothes were on, but word was they were humanoid. For some reason, Maurra tagged this one as male.

With the huge alien backing away, Maurra allowed herself to relax, easing back down onto the small bench that sufficed for a chair. *Another possible disaster averted, thank the stars.* In all her years on the force, she'd never had to subdue an Ellinod before. Was she strong enough to handle one, if it came down to it, she wondered? *There's always the first time to find out.*

Apparently she wouldn't get the chance to find out this time around. Her ruminations were interrupted when the Ellinod got up from his seat and walked out the front door. By his gait she could tell he was a little on the tipsy side. Drunk or not, the alien was still powerful and dangerous. And unpredictable.

A sexy Blois slithered over to her and asked if she wanted another drink. Maurra frowned at the couple of sips left in the bottom of her mug and drew a finger across her throat. The little incident with the Par Mattas had burned away the nice buzz she'd been nursing. Damn. Drawing on her energy always did that, but she should have known better than to come down to the seediest side of town and expect to spend an hour or two in relative quiet.

"Fuck this."

Tossing back the rest of her drink, she paused long enough for the bubbles to explode in her esophagus. Maurra let out a belch, which helped to relieve some of the pressure.

All right. Let me have a decent night's sleep so I can catch tomorrow's flight and arrive back at headquarters looking better than I feel.

It sounded like an acceptable plan. Funny thing, though. The universe had the biggest sense of humor. It especially loved to screw with people's lives.

Gritting her teeth, Maurra left the bar without interference. The night was balmy. Amazingly quiet, considering. What sky she could see overhead was brightly lit with the planet's nine moons in varying phases.

It was because of the quiet that she was alerted to the faint sounds of struggling. Flat, smacking sounds told her someone was getting the shit beaten out of him. What other sounds she could catch were muffled.

There was no hesitation in deciding what she had to do. Being a galactic law enforcement officer was more than a job—it was her life. Her whole life. In fact, it was everything and the only thing in her life. Once she'd taken the vows, and her power had been reinforced, there was no turning back.

The pistol was in her hand before she could think about it as she raced around the side of the building and into the alleyway behind it. When she reached the small back lot, she was already primed to use her psi abilities.

Maurra felt her mouth drop open when she saw the more than half a dozen Kronners furiously beating the hunched-over figure. There was a moment when the sight of a pair of curling horns came into view, and she immediately noticed that one of them flared to the right, like a birth defect, or the result of an accident.

It was the Ellinod from the bar.

The Kronners were trying to take out an Ellinod? For crying out loud, why?

She started to order them to cease, when she hesitated. Yes, the Kronners outnumbered the Ellinod, but she had been wrong about who was getting their asses kicked. In fact, it was somewhat amusing to watch as the little creatures, the tallest of which only came up to the Ellinod's knees, tried to punch and kick the enormous beast into submission.

Maurra smiled. From what she could see, the Ellinod was doing just fine without her, and she leaned back against the wall, crossing her arms over her chest, to watch.

To his credit, the Ellinod was being amazingly gentle with the stick-thin Kronners, tossing them away or brushing them off with swipes of his huge hands. Treating the little creatures like so much dirt coating its uniform.

Fuck this. She wasn't needed here. It was obvious the Ellinod could take care of himself. Still smiling, she turned to leave when her psi senses burned a warning. Maurra whirled around just as another half a dozen Kronners came running in to join the fray, and this time they were carrying stunners.

The unarmed Ellinod no longer had the advantage.

"By the law, I command you to stop!"

She drew a bead on the cluster converging on the Ellinod. The Kronners may have been a fraction of its size, but by bringing in the stunners, they had shifted the odds in their favor. Not to mention outnumbering the Ellinod twelve to one. But the biggest factor forcing her to intervene was the fact that the inebriated beast they were trying to subdue was not able to function at peak efficiency. They had managed to ambush him at a very opportunistic time.

Or maybe they'd planned it that way.

Either way, the Ellinod was giving as good as he got, flinging the Kronners around now like he was wringing his hands of water. His roars of anger were deafening. The attack must have just started when she left the bar, or else she knew she would have heard the ruckus from inside.

"You are ordered by galactic law to stop!" Maurra shouted again, although it wasn't necessary. She'd already given them the prerequisite initial command. She could feel her powers focusing, strengthening, narrowing. Aiming the pistol, she fired.

A field of strong psi powers blasted from her weapon. Bright, blue-white light wrapped around the Kronners, and the creatures shrieked as their nervous systems shut down. The aliens dropped in their tracks.

It took a few seconds for the Ellinod to shove the unconscious Kronners off of him and struggle to his feet. She had hoped to avoid hitting him, but there was always a possibility some residual power would strike him. Maurra could see he was stunned. Hurt. Confused. Angry. Several deep cuts on his arms and chest were bleeding freely. From the way he was breathing heavily, she could tell the attack had taxed his physical resources. Hell, if she didn't have her psi powers, she doubted she would have lasted as long as the Ellinod did.

Holstering her gun, Maurra hurried over to him as he collapsed again to his knees. "Sorry about that. Sometimes a little backlash happens. How do you feel? Do I need to notify medical?"

The Ellinod lifted his head, and she was taken aback by the human looking eyes staring down at her. Light green eyes. Eyes that were still dazed from drink, the beatings, and the psi ray. A trickle of dark blood seeped from a cut in the creature's forehead. The beast tried again to get to his feet when he swayed, almost toppling over.

Automatically, Maurra reached out to help when the beast's eyes widened. She knew instinctively the creature was looking past her. Behind her. He opened his mouth to warn her.

She never had the chance to turn and defend herself when she was hit hard and felt excruciating pain. She was unconscious before she fell to the ground.

Chapter Two
Kronners

Someone is going to pay for this.

She couldn't move. She could barely breathe. Whoever hit her with...whatever it was...

Calm down, Maurra. You're confused and mad, and you're not making a whole lot of sense at the moment. One step at a time. By the book. First things first.

That meant evaluating her physical ability to defend herself. Once she was able to do that, then defending anyone else who had gotten caught in the blast would be her next job.

First things first. Try to move.

Fuck, she couldn't feel the floor, or open her eyes to see if she even was *on* the floor.

She tried wiggling a finger. A toe. Her eyelids. Nothing worked. Nothing obeyed. She was breathing only because the action was relayed automatically from her brain to her lungs. Ditto for the beating of her heart. Unfortunately, getting a message to her brain to coordinate her muscles was impossible.

Fine. Guess I'll have to do it the hard way.

The ray or whatever it was that had hit her had been strong. Strong enough to drop her where she'd stood, and leave her with no memory of what had happened. But nothing was strong enough to negate her psionic abilities. Nothing short of her death could.

Reaching inside herself, Maurra found the sweet core of her power lying patiently like a favorite pet, waiting for her to call to it. As her psionic strength gathered and intensified in front of her forehead, she focused that strength on restoring the rest of her body. Energy surged through her muscles, rushed into her blood, and solidified inside her bones. Within seconds, she had regained feeling in her body and extremities. Her senses had also returned, leaving her nerve endings tingling. That was when she realized she was lying face down on a rough floor. A cold floor.

And she was nude.

Maurra opened her eyes. The lighting was dim, wherever she was. She appeared to be inside some sort of room or cubical, if the semi-opaque corner formed by two walls a few feet away was any indication.

She chanced a longer glance as far as she could, but the wall was too thick to spot anything dangerous. A quick flexing of her fingers reassured her she was back to normal efficiency, or as close to normal as she could get. Her left nipple felt raw, sore, like someone had been manipulating it. She absentmindedly rubbed it with her wrist.

Getting her legs underneath her, Maurra squatted on her heels and took a second, better look around. At the same moment, the walls of her prison solidified, but the lighting remained constant. Someone had realized she was awake, and they had shut her away. Closed her up. Placed her in total isolation. Her pissed attitude rose several notches.

"All right. Who's responsible for all this?"

She got to her feet and clenched her fists. This time she was able to examine her surroundings. Her holding cell was approximately ten meters long by ten meters wide, and ten meters high. A perfect cube. She had no idea where her cube was located. If she did, it might give her some idea as to who had captured her. Who, or what. And thinking of what, she could make a reasonably good guess.

Am I still planetside? No. She could feel a slight vibration under her feet. *Shit, I'm on a ship. Whose ship? The Kronners'? Why would they kidnap me? I've never had a run-in with them.*

"Do you realize that what you did to me is a capital offense?" she cried out. "You attacked a JoJo! An authorized and duly sworn magistrate of galactic law!"

For a second she thought she heard movement outside the walls. Maurra debated whether to chance breaking through the wall with her power. But if she tipped off her attacker, chances were they might overcome her again with whatever ray they had used on her the first time. No. It was better if she held back and waited. Her time would come. It just wasn't now.

"I demand to see who is out there! I can hear you! By galactic order, I command you open this cell and let me out!"

This time there was no mistaking the sound of laughter coming from the other side of the wall. Her pissy attitude started to burn.

"I hope you know that by attacking me, you've opened yourself up to a whole lot of trouble. People have gotten life sentences on prison moons for less!"

The wall to her left began to shimmer. Maurra turned in time to see the whiteness become transparent. On the opposite side were two Kronners, as she had suspected, since they were in the back alley when she'd gone to the defense of the Ellinod. For a moment Maurra wondered what had happened to the Ellinod, when a third Kronner joined his two buddies. She recognized her uniform in his hands.

"Ulraz jouit momvem od!" the third one said in a jeering tone of voice. His friends laughed in response. Mr. Three held up her shirt, particularly the crest which identified her and her status. He waggled the crest at her, taunting her.

The burn became sparks. These idiots had no idea what she could do. But, on the other hand, neither did she know what all they had planned for her, or what they would do to her if she fought them. She eyed the cubicle. This place could be rigged to do just about anything to her if she caused problems.

Give them time, Maurra. Give them enough rope, and they'll eventually hang themselves.

One thing was certain. She was not on Cura-Cura anymore. The almost undetectable vibration under her feet confirmed she was on a ship, and the ship was already in flight. Probably heading back to Kronnaria.

Oh, great. This did not bode well. On the other hand, it could be to her favor. *I'm due back at headquarters in forty spacial hours. If I don't answer roll call, SOP will send out another psi cop to look for me.*

The thought was somewhat reassuring, but in the meantime...

A fourth Kronner appeared from around the corner of her cell. This one carried a bundle of something. Before she could comprehend what it was, the bundle was tossed toward her. She missed the split second the cell wall was down, enabling the bundle to pass through. Maurra cursed herself for the missed opportunity. Apparently her brain was still fuzzy from the aftereffects of their weapon or the drinks she had imbibed.

"In zizi collerero," the Kronner who had tossed the bundle to her ordered. He grasped his chest as if he was holding onto two breasts and jiggled himself. "In zizi collerero."

Now she knew what the bundle was. Maurra went over and picked it up. The shiny black straps were embarrassingly thin. It was a hoochie brace. These Kronners were wanting her to dress up like a common street whore.

Maurra dropped the straps and stood back. "Screw you," she told the quartet. "Give me back my uniform." Without the translator embedded in the uniform, she had no idea what these sleazy aliens wanted. Or were up to.

"In zizi collerero," another one of the Kronners repeated with a bit of anger.

"Fuck your in zizi collerero. Give me back my uniform!"

The instant the Kronner on the far end raised his hand, and she saw the implant in its hand begin to glow, she knew what they had used to subdue her. Well, this time she was ready for it, and she was more than anxious to see which was greater—her psionic power, or their negative neuron ray.

"In zizi collerero!" the angry Kronner ordered. His tone had that ring of finality to it.

Maurra was more than ready. "Go ahead, you little shithead. Show me what you've got!" She punctuated her reply by kicking the hoochie brace across the floor of her cell. She'd rather go nude than put that thing on.

She felt her mouth open in shock when the other three walls of her cell suddenly cleared, and she could see there was one other person being held prisoner like herself.

The Ellinod looked up at her in dazed surprise. His cell must have gone clear like hers, and discovering her there along with him must have been taken him off guard as well. He turned his head to see the Kronners standing beyond the wall, and his face instantly turned gray. Maurra saw him start to go ballistic. His mouth opened to show fierce incisors, and he roared in fury.

Neither of them got the chance to say anything when the Kronner turned and fired at the Ellinod. The pinkish light surrounded the creature, who bellowed in pain instead of anger, and slumped to the floor of his own cube.

"In zizi collerero," the Kronner calmly said again, giving her an irritated look as he pointed to the hoochie suit.

Her temper went combustible. She slammed her hands against the nearly invisible wall of her cell, ready for the jolt that would try to fell her. Focusing her psionic power, Maurra tried to melt her way through.

Two other Kronners lifted their hands, along with the first one, and all three aimed their beams at her. The fourth Kronner kept his hand aimed at the unconscious Ellinod. This time the beam glowed almost black.

"In zizi collerero."

She backed off. It was clear now these little creatures were not above torturing and maybe killing the Ellinod just to get her to dress up as a common prostitute.

Hold off, Maurra. Put the fucking thing on if it'll stop them from attacking him. Remember, your first duty as a JoJo is to protect and defend. Back off, and keep your eyes and ears peeled. There has to be a reason why they kidnapped you. There has to be an explanation why they stripped you and want you to wear that thing.

Maurra reluctantly nodded, hoping they would understand. "All right. You win for now. I'll in zizi collerero."

Picking up the straps, she started to slip them over her head when she had another thought. Why make her put it on when they could have just as easily put it on her themselves when they'd stripped her the first time?

The answer was obvious, she immediately realized. By making her do it herself, they had forced her to bend to their will. Point for the Kronners. Zero for the JoJo. *They must be really loving the odds.*

The outfit included a pair of elbow-length, fingerless gloves and thigh-high boots, both made out of the same cheap, shiny black material. The whole thing was made for show — to wear just long enough for a quick bump-and-grind interlude, and then be ripped off without further ado once she got her customer back to her place for some paid recreation. It was never meant for normal wear.

"Better enjoy it while you can," she murmured softly to the one Kronner who had remained behind to make sure she obeyed entirely. "This game is just beginning, but I play by my own nasty set of rules. Plus, I cheat."

By the time she was finished cinching the last strap, her cell went opaque, leaving her alone in a stark white emptiness. Behind her, she could hear the Ellinod moan softly in pain.

Chapter Three
Introductions

Nearly six hours passed. If there was a side benefit to being psionic, it was the ability to tell time. It didn't matter what planet she was on, or what galaxy she was visiting, she could tell the exact time within seconds. Not all psi cops could do it, and she was better than most who could.

Right now her internal clock was frozen, which meant they were still in space. But the little timekeeper in her brain told her more than five hours had passed since they'd left Cura-Cura.

Her stomach clenched. She was also getting hungry. And cold. The Kronners came from a very warm and humid planet, which meant they kept their ships on the cool side. It would have been all right if she was wearing her uniform, but wearing this hoochie outfit was no better than being bare-ass naked. Long exposure in the chilly room was starting to make her skin shrivel.

She undid the braid behind her head and combed through the thick, dark red mass of hair with her fingers. She pulled some of it over to cover her chest and breasts, and the meager warmth it gave helped. Bringing her knees up to her chin also helped. Sighing loudly, she braced her forehead against her knees.

"Covil mwato?"

The voice was deep. Resonant. Textural, like velvet being dragged across sandpaper. Definitely not the voice of a Kronner.

Wonder if he's cold, too. Like herself, the beast had been nude, which further puzzled her. Kronners wore one-piece outfits, which meant they normally didn't run around in the nude. So why had she and the Ellinod been stripped?

A chilled shudder went through her. Maurra frowned, trying to recall if Ellin was a tropical or frozen world. For that matter, did the Ellinod have a problem with nudity? Or did the Kronners give him some sort of little to nothing outfit to wear, too?

"I don't know what you're saying, but if you're commenting on our situation, I agree with you."

She heard the Ellinod move. It was a subtle shifting, which made her realize she hadn't heard him move before now. Maybe he'd been sleeping off the effects of being rayed, and had just now woken up.

"Iji kuv JoJo?"

All right. That much she could interpret.

"Yeah, I'm a JoJo. My name's Maurra."

"Maurra." There was a slight, silent pause. "Kuvma Safan."

Safan. His name must be Safan.

"Hello, Safan. I wish I could say it was nice to meet you," she quipped.

There was more movement, then she heard the unmistakable sound of peeing. Maurra blinked in surprise. A second later, she realized she had to go, too. A quick glance around showed there wasn't anything in the empty, sterile cube except herself. But at least she had the frosted walls to provide her with a modicum of privacy. Moving over to the furthest corner, she squatted and pulled aside the narrow one-inch strap that ran between her legs. As soon as she was done, she hurried back to the other side of her cell.

"Kleeja. Moromo."

Whatever you say.

The unmistakable sound of a door sliding open got her attention. Maurra jumped to her feet as one wall of her cell went transparent. Three Kronners were standing just inside the entrance to the huge room. One of them Maurra immediately recognized as the graghole who'd thrown the kootchie suit at her.

"Eblee." One that she didn't identify stepped forward until he was close enough to touch the wall of her cell. "Eblee immidoo."

"Fuck you and your immidoo," she spat through gritted teeth.

The lead Kronner gave her an irritated look. He opened his hand to show her a flattish, dull green device about the size of her thumbnail.

"Immidoo karak."

She looked at him quizzically. Obviously the object was for her. What did they want her to do with it? Swallow it? Shove it up her ass?

The wall of her cell began to waver. At the same time, the other two Kronners raised their neuron rays, both set to green. Whatever they had planned for her and that immidoo, they were prepared for her to resist.

Damn right, I'm going to resist. Two one-hundredths of a second, guys. I need less than two one-hundredths of a second. How fast are you with those ray pods? She backed up to the rear wall of her cell. Without her gun to centralize her psionic powers, she'd have to make do with trying to bracket them by hand. She could feel the familiar tingle growing on her forehead. The wall ceased wavering. The way was almost open.

Yeah. You just think *you know how to handle a JoJo.*

Maurra opened her hands, palms facing the opening in her cell, and threw her power at the three Kronners in a wide arc. The psionic force enveloped them in a nice pale pink color, and the Kronners slid unconscious to the floor as soon as it touched them.

She was running for the opening the moment she'd fired. What she wasn't expecting was for a fourth Kronner to be standing off to one side, shielded by the other opaque walls. She barely saw him from the corner of her eye when the neuron ray hit her. It was like running full-tilt into the solid hull of a ship. Her body was thrown into complete rigidity, and she fell unconscious next to the comatose Kronners.

Chapter Four
Explanation

She awoke with a major headache, as if something was digging its digits into her brain. She never got a headache unless something was interfering with her power. Majorly interfering.

Maurra took note of her surroundings. From the quiet she guessed she was back in her cell. On her back. And from the position of her legs and arms, she'd been dumped here.

She tried to send out a mental probe to see if there were any Kronners still around. She was answered with a flash of dark, intense pain that ripped through her spine and up to her neck where it threatened to fry her brain.

Maurra screamed and rolled over, clutching her head in agony. Fortunately the attack had been brief. Unfortunately, echoes of the almost debilitating fire continued to surround her like packs of flesh-eating druloks, ready to pounce on her and shred her into bloody pieces the moment she showed any weakness.

Now she knew what an immidoo was.

Tears coated her cheeks. She was crying. Those fucking Kronners had made her cry, but she had a sneaking suspicion it wouldn't be the last time. Obviously they enjoyed seeing her squirm. She'd heard about some of their sick and twisted games. And it wasn't just a certain few deviant Kronners who relished in watching others being humiliated or tortured. It was the whole damn civilization.

Someone needs to take a squadron of Klasil bombs and just wipe out the whole fucking planet.

The idea made her smile, but it did nothing to stop the minute pricklings inside her skull, as if tiny needles were jabbing her brain. Maurra swiped the tears from her face. As long as she remained calm, the pain was tolerable. Barely.

After six minutes she was finally able to sit up and open her eyes. To her surprise, all of the walls of her cell were transparent. Even the Ellinod's. The big beast-like humanoid was sitting in the middle of his floor and gazing at her with those sea-green eyes. Thick, ridged eyebrows were lowered. The creature looked ready to chew through the walls of his cells if he was forced to. "I was wondering how long it would take you to wake up," he said in that soft, gravelly voice.

Shocked, Maurra stared at him. The creature nodded.

"They put a translator on us." He pointed to his back. "Mine doesn't hurt like yours does, but I think that's because I'm not a psion."

She could hear him speaking in his own tongue. It was no more than a whisper beneath the device interpreting directly into her inner ear.

"I think it's programmed to hurt only when I try to use my power," she told him. Pausing, she checked to make sure she hadn't made a liar out of herself. When no jolt of pain exploded in her head, she gave a slight nod. "Safan, right? Did I understand you earlier?"

The big beast nodded slowly. "My name is Safan."

"Why are you here? I can understand why I got caught up."

If she didn't know any better, she would have sworn she saw a twinkle in his eyes.

"Why do you believe you were taken prisoner, Maurra?" he asked, and smiled.

Damn! That was a twinkle!

"I came to your rescue," she answered. She had been reaching behind her, searching for the immidoo. For a moment she thought her fingertips had brushed across its slick surface, but the Kronners had managed to place it in the one spot she couldn't reach. Maurra sighed with exasperation.

The Ellinod shifted to a more comfortable position. Unlike her, he hadn't been given anything else to wear. She got a brief glimpse of his dick and balls as big as his fist. Yes, he was definitely humanoid. She quickly dropped her eyes and pretended to adjust the tiny strap crossing her breasts. It barely covered her nipples, never mind the areolas.

"I was not their target, Maurra. You were."

Her head jerked up and she stared at him open-mouthed.

"What are you talking about?"

"You're a JoJo. They weren't interested in kidnapping me. They used me to force you to come to my rescue. That had been their intent all along," he told her.

She remembered how earlier the Kronners had threatened to hurt him if she didn't comply with their orders. They knew her top priority was the safety of others. What the Ellinod was telling her made sense.

"But why?"

"You're a JoJo," he repeated gruffly. "You represent the law and everything that stands between them and their ill-gotten gains. That's why they want to humiliate you in every way they can."

"I don't understand." And she still didn't. At least, not completely. "I always have people coming after me for revenge or some other personal vendetta. It comes with the job. Why go to the trouble to use you as bait?" She was trying to blow it off as just another problem day, but deep down she was beginning to think that maybe this time she was in a situation she wouldn't be able to dismiss so easily. Or get out of without losing some skin and a pint or two of blood.

The Ellinod scratched his chest, drawing her eyes to the mountain of muscle. The beast was built. Strong, solid, and powerful. Someone had treated his wounds he'd received planetside. All that was left were a few reddish welts that spotted his skin.

His being there with her made her all the more confused. Why would the Kronners use him as bait to catch her? His people, for all their immense size and strength, were a relatively peaceful race. After centuries of brutal wars, the Ellinod had managed to come to a peaceful if somewhat spotty cease fire when their planet was included in the galactic treaties. Nowadays, most of the planet was involve in mining and trade. Their primary export was billirs, a semi-rare but beautiful stone the Ellinod prided themselves in mining, polishing, and setting into expensive pieces of jewelry. It was the mining which accounted for the beasts continuing to be so well-muscled after their training for warfare had ceased. From what she could see of Safan, he must have spent some time in the mines himself. She wondered how old he was.

"How do you know so much?"

He snorted. "I listen. I watch. I can speak a little Kronnese."

Can speak a little Kronnese? Since when did Ellinod take the time to learn a planet-specific language, much less one from a race of known deviants and con artists? The universal language among traders and merchants was Varonese, the same tongue she used wherever she went.

Maurra glanced back at the doorway to the room. Getting shakily to her feet, she scoped out the entire area as much as she could.

"We're the only ones here," Safan told her, answering her unspoken question.

"We're their only cargo? It doesn't make sense."

"I think I've figured out why," he commented.

"All because of me again?"

"You're worth more to your legion of enemies than you know. Especially if you're presented the right way." He motioned toward the hoochie brace.

The remark irked her. No, it frightened her. Had they kidnapped her because she was a JoJo? Or because of her personally? Did they target Maurra, or the psi cop? "So where are we headed? Back to Kronnaria?"

"I would guess, for the time being."

She started to ask him what he meant by that when the door opened, and this time more than a dozen Kronners filed into the room. At the same time, both her and the Ellinod's cells began to move.

Toward each other.

Maurra squatted, fingertips on the floor to help keep her balance. When the two platforms met, there was a hiss and a gentle bump. The walls between them wavered and disappeared. She and the creature were now technically in one large holding pen. She eyed the little aliens circling them.

"Let me guess. Each one of them is holding one of those neuron rays," she stated flatly.

"They're preparing the stage," Safan murmured.

She shot the Ellinod a guarded look. "What stage?"

He nodded and glanced upward. "Do you see anything along the walls, just below the ceiling?"

Maurra looked up at what he was talking about. Every few meters, it appeared as though something sparkled. "What are those?"

"I'm willing to bet they're video scopes."

"So? Every transport ship has a camera in the hold, to watch over their cargo."

"This isn't one camera, Maurra. I counted more than twenty of them. I think they're vidding us."

"What?"

He started to say more when the Kronner she thought of as the leader of this bunch of miscreants stepped forward. He made certain to show her the ray in his hand first.

"You will do as we say," he said, waving the ray at her. Like it was when the Ellinod spoke to her, the Kronner's chattering voice sounded faintly in the distance when the translator spoke to her. The damn things even included vocal nuances and inflections. *These people use top-of-the-line equipment,* she realized, and wondered what other surprises they might have in store.

"Do as we say and there will be no pain," another Kronner joined in.

Maurra threw him a dirty look. No pain? Did they mean for the Ellinod or for her?

"You're looking at life without parole on Dumanbarti Four," she told him, using her best professional voice. Getting back up, she made it a point to turn around slowly and look each Kronner in the face. A few were nervous, but the majority had that evil glint in their tiny pink eyes she easily recognized. "I am a JoJo. I represent the law in this quadrant of the Nebu Hollum galaxy. By kidnapping me, you have violated not just galactic law, but the laws of the twelve treaties of the universe. At the least, you all will be sentenced to life on the prison moon. And I can assure you your life won't last long."

Another Kronner stepped forward. "We do not care for your laws. Your laws do not affect us."

Maurra blinked. The law didn't affect them? Kronnaria was well inside the boundaries set by the galactic council. Every world included had agreed to and signed the treaties, promising to abide by the terms listed. And that's the way it had been for the last fourteen hundred or so years. What did he mean, they didn't care for the laws?

"According to my orders, Kronnaria is part of this quadrant. You are under my jurisdiction, so therefore you are obligated to obey the laws," she advised.

The second Kronner grinned. It reminded her of small, evil-minded boys who enjoyed torturing small animals and causing havoc, regardless of the consequences. Their primary goal was and would always be to see how much misery they could cause for others.

"No one here cares about your threats, JoJo. Your laws do not affect us. You will play by our rules because you have no choice."

The other Kronners laughed at the joke. Maurra raised an eyebrow and glowered at them to show her disdain. Behind her she could hear the Ellinod growl in contempt. "Keep laughing, you little pricks," she said. "We'll see who wins in the end."

"We already know who will win," the first Kronner said. "We will win because you will do as we say."

"Other psi cops will come looking for me when I don't return to headquarters."

"They will not know where to find you. And those of us who know..." He giggled. The sound rasped across her nerves. "This is your fate, JoJo. You will never be allowed to leave to tell the others." He motioned at his back. "You will never leave because we will not let you."

Maurra gritted her teeth. "Pretty wishful thinking."

The little alien dismissed her anger. "You may keep your anger. It entertains us."

Entertains us? Maurra glanced again at the little glittering portholes encircling them.

"No more talk, JoJo," Kronner number one stated. "The others are waiting. You will obey us now."

"Screw you," she shot at them.

Kronner number two shook his head and grinned. "No. That is what *you* will do." Pointing to the Ellinod, he said, "Fuck the beast, JoJo, or else we will hurt him bad."

Chapter Five
Revenge

Tramer Vol Brod remained in his seat and stared at the multitude of screens displayed on the wall before him when the little Kronner leader came into the cabin. "How are we doing on subscriptions?" he casually inquired before the alien could say anything.

"We are up to four point three billion subsonic payees," Mincred answered gleefully. "We just went over eight point six billion for the holo subscriptions!"

Vol Brod's eyes dropped to the display in question. Directly in front of him on the holo platform was a 3-D representation of what the videos were showing. Subscribing to the direct video feed was costing each audience member a disgustingly high fee, but going holo was more than twice that. From the looks of things, after his subscribers got a taste of what he had to offer, he suspected they would be more than willing to cough up for the more exclusive—not to mention more intimate—feed. He smiled.

"Very good. And the JoJo, is she rebelling?"

"Oh, yes," Mincred nodded. "She is going to be a hard one to tame."

"I don't want her tamed!" Vol Brod yelled, suddenly whirling around in his seat to face the Kronner. "I don't want her *tamed!* I want her to obey our wishes, but I want to keep that fire alive! Do you understand me? Our subscribers aren't paying to see her broken. They want to see her fight! They want to see her defy us and rebel! They want to see her humiliated and de-humanized, but they don't want her defeated. Am I getting this across to you, Mincred?"

The Kronner grinned maliciously. Good. He was getting across.

"You're damn right we're rebellious! That's what makes people like me and her so valuable to people like you. It's my idea making you all filthy rich, and it's her that's bringing in the money."

Setting this whole thing up had cost him every credit to his name, and plenty more from his backers. But he had promised them they would get a show that would make them all quadrillionaires, and so far things were working out as planned. The only hard part had been overcoming the JoJo and getting her aboard the specially outfitted Kronner craft. The Ellinod... Vol Brod dismissed the hulking beast without further thought. He had needed a species humanoid enough to be able to perform with the JoJo. Initially he had eyed one of the Par Mattas, along with its two cocks, but once he'd set his eyes on the Ellinod, Vol Brod couldn't believe his good fortune. He had debated whether the Par Matta and its tentacles might turn off some of his clients. Yet as soon as the Ellinod had strode into the bar, Vol Brod knew the monstrous creature was exactly what he'd been seeking.

Other than the beast's skull-shaped head and massive, curving horns, it was humanoid enough. Its body was massive and muscular. Every part. Vol Brod had known instinctively that the creature was a male, and once the Kronners had stripped it, he had congratulated himself on his choice.

The Ellinod was perfect for fornicating with the JoJo.

"Is there anything else you need me for?" Mincred asked. It was clear the little alien wanted to return to the holding area where he could watch the fun in person. That perk was part of the Kronners' share of the wealth, along with exclusive rights to the vids once everything was over, as well as a percentage of the profit. In the meantime, Vol Brod was the mastermind behind the whole thing, and he was the man running the show.

"You can go. Keep me informed of our subscriber accounts," he told the little alien.

The little Kronner grinned and practically skipped out of the cabin. The more subscriptions that came in, the more money everyone made.

And I will have the greatest revenge. Vol Brod laughed.

He would relish every bit of it as the sordid scenario played itself out.

Chapter Six
Realization

Maybe the translator didn't interpret that right. "You want me to *what?*" Maurra demanded, giving the Kronners a look of shock and disgust.

"Fuck the Ellinod."

She turned to look at the beast to see a look of absolute surprise on its face. She was about to respond when Safan got to his feet and faced the little aliens.

"There is a heavy penalty for interspecies fornication," he told them. "Because of the vast mutations caused by interbreeding in the past, and because those mutations always resulted in disease-prone or schizophrenic generations, reproduction was banned by the Galactic Council. The laws are clear on this. They are mentioned in the twelve treaties."

Kronner number one snickered. "We told you. The treaties mean nothing to us. You are here for a purpose." Shiny pink eyes darted over to include Maurra. "Both of you are here to entertain us. And the others."

"Others?" The word was out of her mouth before she realized it. Again, she glanced at the vidding equipment overhead. "What are you? Some kind of sick voyeur?"

The Kronners laughed. "There are many like us," Number Two explained. "They want to see you hump the

Ellinod. They want to see you grovel. And they are paying us a lot of creds for the privilege to watch."

"Yeah. A *lot* of creds," another Kronner emphasized with a snicker.

Without warning, the Ellinod roared and charged the walls of his cage. The Kronners reacted instinctively, literally falling all over themselves as they tried to get out of the creature's way.

Safan hit the wall with his chest and arms. There was a loud boom, and a flash of light that nearly blinded her. When the light finally died down, the Ellinod was still standing, but he was dazed from the backlash. Wavering on his feet. Fighting to stay conscious.

Once the Kronners were aware that the cell wall had held, they gathered back around, and Number Two ambled back up. "You cannot escape. Your attempts will just make the barrier stronger."

"He's right."

Maurra turned to the Ellinod, who gave a weak gesture toward the cell wall. "I felt it sap something out of me. If I keep hitting it, I think it will eventually drain me of everything."

A giggle brought her attention back to the Kronner. She gave him her best psi cop glare, which made the little alien take an involuntary step back. "You haven't won," she told him. "Not by a long shot. I will get out of here. Somehow, someway, I'm getting free. And when I do, I promise I won't make your life worth living."

The threat made the little alien laugh, albeit nervously. "That is good! Fight, JoJo! Fight us!" He became suddenly serious. "Now, quit wasting time. Fuck the Ellinod. Now."

Maurra didn't have to look over at Safan to know that he was reining in his anger just like she was. "I can't fuck him," she objected hotly. "He's too big! We won't fit!"

An obnoxious smile smeared over the Kronner's face. "Your objections amuse us, but they will do you no good. If you do not take the Ellinod, we have a Par Matta sitting in the next hold. Perhaps you would rather take it on instead?"

At the mention of the Par Matta, Maurra shuddered, then cursed herself for her weakness. But the thought of that thing's tentacles sliding over her made her body go cold. The slime-coated tentacles were one thing, but she also knew the males had two penises to doubly penetrate their females. At least an Ellinod was humanoid with one, even if it was immense.

The Kronner eyed her closely. "What say you, JoJo? Do I go get the Par Matta?"

"No," Maurra hastily answered. At least her voice didn't betray her revulsion.

Nodding, the Kronner lifted his neuron ray. "Then begin. But remember, if you fail to please us, we will be forced to punish you."

"What about protection? At least give us protection so I don't get pregnant!"

Their laughter set her teeth on edge. "You don't deserve protection."

The Kronner stepped back until he had rejoined the circle of other Kronners just as the lights inside the hold went out. All except for the four bright lights on the hover vids covering all four corners of the rectangular cell. Maurra glanced down to see that beneath them the cell floors also brightened. As Safan had mentioned earlier, the stage was being set, and both actors were in the spotlight. If there was anything to be grateful for, Maurra realized, it was the fact that the Kronners were standing just beyond the darkness where she couldn't see them.

She flexed her fingers, unsure as to what to do next. Although chances were slim her genes and those of the Ellinod might be compatible enough to create new life, the chance still remained. Not to mention a hundred other problems that could arise.

"Maurra."

Looking up, she saw the Ellinod gesturing for her to join him. He had seated himself on the floor, legs crossed. From where she stood she couldn't see his genitals.

Could an Ellinod get it up for someone of her species?

Slowly, Maurra walked over to the beast and sat down in front of him. "If I refuse to do what they say, they'll hurt you. They'll keep hurting you, and you could die, but they wouldn't care. They'd just bring in another species like that Par Matta. And if I refuse the Par Matta, there's no telling what else they'll kidnap and throw in here with me." A heavy weight had descended on her chest, making her work for every breath. Her face felt full. Stuffy. Her eyes stung, and her skin felt hot. She gritted her teeth as her anger burned. "They have me caught between two impossible outcomes. Do I screw you, and break the treaties, knowing they're broadcasting this to heavens know how many solar systems? Or do I let them openly murder you and others? Because if I stand by and let you die, I'll also be breaking the laws that I've sworn to uphold."

"You want me to answer that?" he gruffly asked. "Or don't you already know the answer?"

Maurra closed her eyes, unaware of the tears falling from her lashes. She tried to swallow, failed, cleared her throat, and tried again. "How many times do you think they're going to make us do this?" she whispered as she felt him take her hand. It was very rough, but surprisingly, it was also warm.

"We cannot let ourselves think that far ahead," Safan said. "For now, we must somehow get through this. Maybe, if we're lucky, they'll let us go when we reach Kronnaria."

Her eyes snapped open, and she found herself staring into those so-human-looking green eyes. In their depths she saw his own anger barely held in check. "You know as well as I do that once we get there, this won't be over. If they're making money off of this, like they say they are, and I have every reason not to doubt them, they'll continue with this sick escapade."

He tilted his head. "What makes you say that?"

"They don't want to just humiliate me, Safan. They want to see me destroyed in as many ways as they can. My body, my mind, and my spirit. Once they've done that, then they'll stop this. I'm sure of it." She glanced out at the darkness where the Kronners were keeping unusually quiet. "At some point they've developed a deep-seated hatred of JoJos. It looks like I've won the lottery."

"But there's always the chance you'll be freed to go home after you give in to them," he stated.

Maurra shook her head. "They'll never allow me to go home. Don't you see? They've made this my fate, and the only way I'll be free of it is when I'm dead."

Chapter Seven
Reaction

"The sooner we do this, the sooner they'll leave."

Maurra turned around to look out at the darkness just beyond the lights illuminating their cell. The vid cameras she could accept, albeit grudgingly. They were silent eyes. The Kronners, however, were a live audience. She and the Ellinod were on display for them to taunt and harass, and to laugh over. Jeering. Cheering. Urging them on. Their participation would be no different than the audiences' behavior in hoochie shows over in the seedier parts of some planets, where women took high money to fuck any creature with a penis, and do it in front of witnesses to prove she'd earned the money square and fair.

I'm not doing it to earn money. I'm doing it to earn our lives.

Yes, but you're still breaking the law, her conscience argued. *Isn't defending the law worth the price of life?*

Defending the law should never take a life. Never! she countered.

An enormous hand reached over and took hers. Maurra glanced down to see it completely close over hers. It was warm and hard, and it wasn't much different from the touch of a human hand. But the arm attached to the hand was equal to three of hers.

"Maurra. Come."

He pulled her down to the floor and made her sit facing him. The hand released hers and grabbed her chin instead, turning her gaze away from what was outside the cell walls and toward him.

Maurra stared at the creature. She could count on one hand how many lovers she'd had in the past. She couldn't even call them lovers. Realistically, they had been nothing more than casual flings. Willing partners whenever she had felt the urge, or when her loneliness had become too much to bear. None of them had lasted more than one or two beddings. None of them had touched her in any way emotionally. They had been men of power, or men with a pretty face and body. Men who had been more than eager to see if screwing a psion was the thrill rumors promised it would be.

She gave a mental shrug. Maybe it was, but not for her. She'd never gotten off on the trysts, but at least she'd taken care of that momentary physical need.

Now I can add one more bed buddy to my list. Perhaps my last one.

He may be her last one, but this one would be her only lover not of her own kind, or of her own species. She gave the creature another good stare, especially at the equipment lying between his knees, and wondered if the Ellinod was as repulsed by the whole ordeal as she was.

"Safan, how many of your women have you bedded?"

He squinted at her. "Bedded or fucked?"

"Oh, there's a difference?" Maurra felt one side of her mouth rise in spite of the circumstances.

"Yes, there is. When I bed a woman, it is to sleep. To find comfort and rest in her companionable warmth and in her arms. When I fuck, it is to scratch my cock until I'm able to relieve the pressure in my balls. And when I'm satisfied with both, I send the woman on her way."

"Then you've never mated? Never found a woman to bear your children?"

Safan paused, and Maurra got the impression he was holding something back.

"Never mind," she said. "You're right. Let's get this over with. What do you want me to do?"

There. There was that twinkle again in his green eyes. What was he thinking?

"You can begin by removing your clothing."

She undid the hoochie brace and tossed it at the corner of the cell. If she was lucky, she'd never have to put it on again.

Safan reached over and guided her down to the floor, then spread her thighs in front of him. He stared at the juncture between her legs for a moment.

"Talk to me, Safan. Don't keep me in suspense." She was half-serious, half-jesting with him. It was all she could manage since she was shuddering inside. Her skin felt hot and dry. Every muscle rippled like water, and her stomach threatened to throw her into dry heaves.

"I thought your species was furred between your legs," he commented.

This time his comment actually made her smile. Furred? "We are, but I had mine permanently removed some time ago."

"Why?"

"My uniform fits better. Sometimes the hairs would get caught in the weave. Or when I climbed or jumped, they'd get pinched or pulled."

His thick, stubby fingers tentatively touched her, running from her inner thigh to her lower lips. The cautious examination was gentle.

"You are soft. I have never felt such softness." Glancing up at her, Safan admitted, "Ellinod women are not furred. Neither are they soft like this."

"Some men equate softness with undesirability," she told him. "They want firmness. To them, they think anything soft is weak."

His hand rested on her mound. "I cannot envision you as being weak. JoJos are not weak, and have never been known to be weak. The strength of your power and your character is worthy enough for me to call you Ellinod." Running a warm thumb over her pubic lips, he said, "You will have to work on me to make me hard enough to penetrate you. And you will have to guide me to let me know what pleasures you, so you do not present any resistance."

"What pleasures *me?*" The words popped out of her before she was aware of saying them.

Safan gave a slow nod. "It must be pleasure, Maurra, or else your body will try to reject me."

He was right. Apparently, he was much more experienced at this sort of thing than she was. She acknowledged to herself, *Let him lead.*

He rubbed his palm over her again. "What would be easier for you? On top of you, or from behind?"

On top of you, or from behind? Maurra realized with a start that although she knew there were multiple ways and positions her people could fornicate, she had only fucked using one of them.

"I'll lie down. You lie on top of me," she answered. "It's the way I'm most familiar with."

Another twinkle glittered in his eyes. "If I lie on top of you, I will crush you, and they will be out a JoJo."

The visual image of her lying bloody, flattened, and nude beneath him struck her as funny, and Maurra began to giggle. The giggle quickly morphed into laughter, albeit nervous laughter. Unable to stop, she sat up and reached for him, pressing her forehead to his massive chest where she could hear the steady drumbeat of his heart. The Ellinod waited patiently for her to calm, and when she did, she found herself almost nose-to-nose with the beast.

This close she could catch his scent. It was a wild smell. Rich and earthy. Somewhat unusual, but not off-putting. His skin was a blanket of dark, muddy colored textures. Mostly a dark gray, becoming darker, almost black in some areas, or shading into browns in others. She touched a sunken cheek to find it leathery, but it wasn't an unpleasant feeling. The forehead was high, forming a crest where his two enormous, curved horns jutted out. The brow ridges were thick, the nose slightly hooked. And his lips... She gently fingered the full lower lip. His upper one was thin, almost to the point of nonexistence.

"Does your species kiss?"

"Not to the extent yours does," he replied gruffly. His voice sent small waves of warmth through her with its sound, even through the translator. She vaguely wondered if he was manipulating his voice to make himself appear less intimidating.

Slowly, hesitantly, she leaned in and lightly touched his lips with hers. There was no movement, no tasting or tonguing, and yet Maurra couldn't remember when she'd ever felt a more sensual kiss. The revelation shocked her, and she pulled back to stare into his eyes for another moment before Safan moved away.

"How do I...how do I turn you on? Does this help?"

She reached down between them where his penis lay along the floor. It was long and flaccid. Deflated. Unlike a human male's, it retained its length, just not its girth. When she slowly ran her nails lightly down its side, it began to swell. Where it had curved, it straightened out, much like a hose coming under pressure.

"That feels good," Safan admitted.

She picked it up and tried to hold it with one hand, but its enlarging thickness was too big for her to close her fingers around it. The large, dark-colored, helmet-shaped head was hidden beneath the foreskin, which she pulled away. Thick blue-black veins extended down his erection, to disappear at the root. The cock pulsed in her palm as it continued to fill out and thicken, but it didn't increase in length, unlike the penises of human males, which both shrunk and retracted when not excited. She ran her short nails over the soft, almost suede-like skin, and a tremor went through him. Maurra toyed with the idea of taking him into her mouth when Safan took her by the shoulders and pushed her down to the floor.

To her surprise, he propped himself above her until he was an immense wall of flesh caging her, looming over her. His arms were braced on either side of her head, his knees outside her thighs. Towering as he was above her, he reminded her of a massive thundercloud. Had circumstances been different, he would have been a terrifying figure. But right now, she reminded herself that he was just as much a victim as she was, and she wondered what he was thinking at this moment.

Something prodded between her legs. Maurra glanced down to see his erection nearly fully engorged. Stiff and extended, the tip of it pressed at the juncture at her mound. His hips moved slightly, and a few inches of the thick rod disappeared into the V.

Her breath caught in her throat. His erection had brushed across her clit and was still lying against it. The heavy pulse of blood in his veins throbbed next to her sensitive flesh. She looked up into heavy-lidded green eyes and could see the Ellinod was also feeling...something.

Safan moved his hips again, drawing his rigid dick slightly upward before pressing down another inch. The rasping motion sent a shiver through her. Without thinking, Maurra reached down with one hand, slid her fingers around his thick girth, and began masturbating herself with it.

Immediately her juices started flowing, making the motion smoother. Above her, Safan groaned softly but didn't move.

"You are getting wetter," he whispered.

"Yeah."

Amazingly, it felt good. It felt...exciting.

Damn her. Maurra cursed herself as she continued to rub them together. He was warm and getting warmer. Hot. His rough skin abraded her clit without scouring it. She parted her legs and increased the pressure as her cream coated the insides of her thighs and mound, and made his rod slick.

A fire was building inside her. Maurra wondered if the Kronners would be satisfied if she came manually. Hell, would they even be able to tell the difference, whether or not he penetrated her?

The Ellinod suddenly dropped to one elbow. The action startled her, and without thinking Maurra threw up a psi shield to protect herself. It was an instinctive reaction. One drilled into her from years of training and survival skills. Unfortunately, it was the wrong thing to do.

A sword of pure, white hot agony sliced into her brain. Maurra screamed and clutched her head with both hands as her body went into shock. She was barely aware of the Ellinod rising up and roaring his anger toward the cameras, toward their enemy hiding in the anonymity of darkness.

"Take it off her! Take the device off her! You're killing her!"

Several seconds passed without an answer. Gradually, the pain began to lessen, leaving her numb, but residual pain continued to throb around the interior of her skull like someone had placed a band around her head and continued to tighten it.

Safan growled again. It rumbled low and deep within his chest. He turned to look back down at her when a new voice, a male voice, came over the speakers.

"We will not take off the device. We're not stupid."

He whirled back around. "Take it off her!" he repeated. "Take it off, or she could scramble her brains, and all your preparations will be for nothing."

Maurra pulled her hands away from her eyes to see the Ellinod towering over her. His whole body was white with anger, and his heavy dick bobbed like a thick arm above her belly. He was breathing heavily, but he had managed to temper his voice. He didn't want to incur any of the Kronners' wrath upon her.

He was protecting her, the same way she had tried to protect him.

"Then perhaps you need to teach her not to use her psi powers. That way she won't be subject to any more pain. Now...get on with fucking her. My customers are becoming impatient."

The Ellinod looked down at her. She could read defeat in his face. Honest defeat. They could not rely on her powers to free them from this, which meant their only other possible means of escape would have to be through him. But other than his great brute strength, Safan had no powers.

"How is the pain?" he whispered down to her.

She swallowed back the acidic phlegm gathered in her throat. "Better."

"Enough to continue?" He gave the nearest camera an angry look. "They won't let us stop until we're done."

"Yeah."

"Can you handle an orgasm?" the beast asked.

Maurra stared at him in surprise. The Ellinod nodded.

"It is the least I can do to repay you for your sacrifice. Close your eyes."

She started to reply when Safan again reared over her, caging her with his body, but this time she didn't react to his sudden movements when he dipped his enormous horned head toward her face.

Chapter Eight
Release

He licked her. A slow, wet, warm slide with his rough tongue starting below her rib cage, and running across her upper chest toward her neck.

"Close your eyes."

Taking a deep breath, Maurra closed her eyes and tried to let herself go. It was damn near impossible. Her whole body strummed with unreleased tension, with worry, with anger. With the threat of her life and the life of the Ellinod hanging over them. Or rather, with the threat staring at them with heavens knew how many video eyes.

Safan moved a strand of long red hair off her nipples. She was barely aware of it until he lowered himself down to her belly and began another slow ascent over her skin with his warm, wet tongue. As it rasped over her breast and nipple, an undeniable jolt of desire surged through her, surprising her and making her gasp. Her eyes flew open to see the Ellinod watching her intently.

"Close your eyes."

She quickly shut them again, and realized with surprise that the last vestiges of pain had vanished. She waited for where he would lick her next as her body gradually unwound. She didn't have long to wait.

This time he started below her navel, twirling the tip of his tongue around the puckered dimple. A sizzling heat began to ignite between her thighs, and Maurra remembered how good his dick had felt rubbing across her clit. The tongue moved upward toward her other breast, and by the time he reached it, her nipples were hardened tips. Safan cupped the breast with one hand and drew it into his mouth. It was like enclosing her flesh in an electrical storm.

The sizzle burst into flame deep within her womb and threw her body into shock. Maurra gasped, not believing what she was feeling, and unable to understand how the Ellinod was able to get such a reaction from her. Her arms flew upward, her hands seeking his head, his face, when her fingers found his wide horns. Without thinking, she stroked them, and Safan groaned loudly.

"Again."

The sweet burning between her legs was making her wet all over again. In addition, getting him off was working like an aphrodisiac on her. Wrapping her fingers around each hard protrusion and running her hands up and down them was no different than stroking his erection. Safan's grunt of lust verified it.

"I must take you now," he almost growled. She didn't answer as his hands were already spreading her legs, and she felt him positioning her. Reluctantly she let go of his horns as the Ellinod sat back on his heels.

She couldn't open her eyes to look at what she knew was happening. She was too afraid that staring at his swollen dick would kill whatever passion he'd started flowing through her. When the hot head nudged her opening, she wasn't expecting Safan to reach down and begin vibrating one finger against her swollen clit.

Desire like the richest spice rippled through her, melting her muscles and her last reservations. The bulbous helmet of his erection slipped inside her, and immediately her body arched at the invasion.

The finger continued to thrum, making her wetter and hotter as white lights flashed behind her eyelids. Another inch of him slipped inside, and this time the rough outer skin dragged thickly through her inner channel, heightening sensitive nerve endings and firing them off like rockets. She cried out without realizing it as the Ellinod pushed another couple of inches into her.

He was going to rip her apart, one way or another. She knew it without question. There was no way she could contain all of him. She had known it from the moment she'd first seen his oversized genitals. Yet, she couldn't deny the feelings running rampant through her. There was no way she could compare screwing an Earth Sapien with what was happening to her now. It was both overwhelming and exquisite. It was perfect, as if it was meant to be. Worse, damn her for what she was feeling.

"More." The word came out as a gasp, a squeak. A plea.

The Ellinod dragged her hips upward, over his thighs. His erection sank in another inch, but this time he gently pulled out of her. Not far, but enough to let her juices slide over his flushed dick to ease further insertion. There was a rumbling sound emanating from his chest, and Safan bent over, shoving half his length inside her. It was too much.

Pain.

Maurra screamed, her hands reaching between her legs. The Ellinod caught her wrists and held them away from their connection. He gave his pelvis a jerk, trying to adjust for the tight fit, and finally released her arms. She never sensed him leaning back over her until his mouth and hand closed simultaneously over her right breast.

The Ellinod suckled. The strong pull on her nipple was hard, demanding, and unbelievably hot. At the same time he pushed more of himself into her. Then withdrew. In. Out. Slow. Steady. Rhythmically. Gently, almost tenderly. Every time inserting another few centimeters.

He was fitting inside her, but just barely. He was stretching her, filling her. She could not begin to imagine how tight she must be for someone his size.

Reaching up, she found his horns hovering above her head. He was working her breasts in wild and wonderful ways, nibbling and scraping them with teeth that could terrify an army of warriors. Pulling on her nipples so roughly, she could feel the tug deep inside her channel. Reaching up, she began to stroke his horns again, keeping pace with his lunges. The Ellinod snorted and paused, and she felt a tremor go through him. There was a soft, wet sucking sound as his mouth released one breast.

"More."

She adjusted her grip on his horns and started stroking them harder, faster, until her fists were pounding against his skull. Safan groaned as his body reacted to the erotic stimulation. He froze to let the pleasure wash over him. A moment later, he continued his assault on her body, increasing both his speed and penetration with each thrust of his hips. Ramming his dick inside her with almost animalistic intensity.

Almost immediately she felt the first whirlwind rise within herself, and Maurra realized she was going to have an orgasm. It wouldn't be her first, but it would be her first with a partner. Correct that—it would be her first doing it the old way. The natural way. The way intended by creation.

Stop thinking about it and take it, she sternly told herself. *Enjoy it.*

Enjoy it!

She forgot about the vids. She forgot about the cage, and the Kronners, and the circumstances as to why she was there. More than that, she forgot about the fallout, should the authorities learn what she and the Ellinod had done.

There was no there. There was no here. There was only now. And Safan. And his hard, heavy cock tearing her apart bit by bit with more unbelievable pleasure than her body could take. And when her release shot through her, totally disintegrating her body and soul, she screamed.

The Ellinod continued to pump her, grinding himself into her as deeply as he could without physically damaging her. His breath was coming in gasps. His hands were shaking so badly, his claws were starting to draw blood where they clung to her thighs.

Suddenly, he jerked his head up and turned his face to the ceiling, ripping his horns from her hands. A bellowing roar filled the cell to the point where she thought her eardrums would burst.

Inside her channel she felt an unmistakable pulsing, rhythmic and strong. He was pouring himself into her, coming in continuous hard spurts. The Ellinod growled again, shuddered, and barely managed to avoid crushing her when he fell forward. His hands slammed against the floor. There was a grunt and a whoosh of air exiting his lungs, followed by silence.

He was still inside her but she could tell it was over. His member was deflating within her channel. It was a curious feeling, sensing him shrinking rather than withdrawing.

She was riding on air, in a ship with zero gravity. Floating free while her body tingled in the aftermath. When he finally pulled out of her, she wasn't prepared for him to roll onto his side and pull her along with him.

The cell faded. The lights from the vids dimmed. Her consciousness continued to sink into oblivion when a voice overhead stated, "Excellent performance. I am pleased. For that, you have earned the right to eat."

If anything more was said, she never heard it.

Chapter Nine
Understanding

She smelled food. The warmth that had been at her back was gone, leaving her chilled and feeling oddly isolated. In fact, there was little she could detect, much less hear.

Maurra slowly rolled over onto her stomach. Her muscles ached, but the worse pain was the soreness between her thighs. But all of that she could easily forget and forgive with the memory of what had happened.

She froze and fought the nauseous wave rolling in her belly. It wasn't the memory of what had occurred between her and the Ellinod that made her stomach clench. It was the sudden realization that she no longer had any sense of time. How long had she been out? How long ago did they screw? Hours? Days?

Her head felt fogged up, dense, as if she had been hit with a disease or illness, but she knew her power was still there. She had not lost her psi abilities. They had merely been tempered to the point where she was no more powerful than a sick child. Her powers were still hers to command, except she could no longer command them. If she did, there would be nothing but excruciating pain and agony. The Kronners had managed to chain her in order to bend her to their will. And if she had any chance of escaping, the first thing she had to do was find a way to remove the translation device from her back in order to use her powers.

At that moment, the Ellinod was the stronger and more capable of the two of them. Somehow she had to find a way to talk to him without the Kronners listening in. Together they had to find a way or a means of escaping. The Kronners were not going to win. Maybe they had won the battle this time, but they had not won the war.

They will not win this war. They will never win this war.

Lifting her head, Maurra finally found the source of food she'd been smelling. There was a small tray lying on the floor at the far end of the cell. She also noticed that the walls of the cell were opaque again. The Ellinod was no longer with her. Had the Kronners moved the Ellinod back to his own cell? Or had the Ellinod left of his own accord? What if the Kronners had let him go, now that he'd fucked her?

She made her way over to the small tray. It held several mounds of small greenish and blackish matter, none of which looked appetizing. She stuck her finger into one lumpy, gritty pile. It was cold. It was also bland, she discovered when she licked her finger, but it had to be somewhat nourishing if the Kronners gave it to her to eat. Maurra quickly scarfed down everything on the tray, and tried to ignore the consistency and lack of taste.

With her hunger alleviated, the next thing she needed was a bath, or at least something warm like a compress for her bruises. Come to think of it, a wet cloth would be very welcome. She was covered in dried sweat, and she was sticky, especially between her thighs.

Thinking of her thighs, Maurra could still feel residual twinges, reminding her of what she and the Ellinod had done. If she reached down and touched her pubic lips, she knew she would find them swollen and tender. If Safan was still here, how long would it be before the Kronners forced them to perform again for their vid subscribers? How much time would the Kronners give them to recuperate?

Her thoughts were interrupted by a sudden noise at the other end of the cell, drawing her attention in that direction. A window opened, and little hand shoved a mug across the floor before disappearing through a tiny slit that closed immediately behind it. Maurra crawled over to find the mug contained water. She quickly drank the contents and left the mug by the wall before retreating back to her corner of the cell.

Of everything about her circumstances, the thing she hated the most was the fact that she felt completely powerless, lost, and confused. Her psi powers were more than a form of protection or a weapon. They heightened her senses and made her more aware of everything around her. Without them she felt like she was groping in the dark with plugs in her ears.

But I'm not completely helpless. I still have my physical strength and my training. Plus, I can still think for myself.

She paused. Maybe this was a good thing. Maybe something good would come out of this whole ordeal. As a psi cop, she had always depended entirely on her power to enforce the law. She rarely, if ever, used her own physical abilities to help restrain criminals. Same for having to out-think or outwit them. Faced now with not having her power to fall back on, she had no choice but to rely on her most basic self.

There was a bright spot, however. She knew she had an ally in the Ellinod. A very strong, almost brutish alien species that was known for its strength and intelligence.

Curling up on the floor, Maurra tried to get comfortable. She needed to rest. Unfortunately, as exhausted as she felt, her mind wouldn't stop thinking. Thoughts and ideas and plans swirled around in her head. She rolled over and brought her knees up, hoping to conserve heat.

Rest, Maurra. You need rest. Oh, damn. What I wouldn't give for a blanket.

"Maurra?"

The voice was soft and nearby. On the other side of the wall next to her. Maurra moved closer to the wall.

"Maurra?"

"Safan?"

"Did you eat?"

"Yes. You?"

"Yes." There was a pause, then he asked, "How do you feel?"

She tried to read him. It was an automatic response, and she was rewarded with a twinge in her temple, reminding her that using any part of her psi abilities would not be pleasant. Instead, she forced herself to listen to the tone of his voice, and from the sound of it he didn't sound happy. Neither did he sound angry. She could be wrong, but he almost sounded...sad.

"I'm sore, but..." But what? Maurra paused. She was about to tell him it didn't matter. That this whole ordeal no longer mattered, and by all the stars in the heavens she didn't understand why not.

When had she stopped worrying about what she was being forced to do?

Because it's over. Because it happened, and there's no reason to think any more about it. I've broken the law, and there will never be any way I can go back and undo it.

What's done is done.

She heard movement on the other side of the wall. "But what?" the Ellinod asked.

"But I'll live." It sounded like a lame response, but at least it was the truth.

The Ellinod snorted. "Yes, we are both still alive, but for how long? Maurra, you and I know this cannot go on for very much longer. Sooner or later we will be separated, and either you or I will be given a new challenge. Maybe a new fuck partner. Who can tell? But at some point it will all end.

I'm afraid that point will come only when one of us, or both of us, are dead."

Maurra lowered her face and pressed her forehead to the cold floor. He was correct. He was as much aware of the fact as she was that this whole ordeal was only temporary. How temporary, they couldn't begin to guess. That was why it was imperative that they find a way out of this mess as soon as possible.

"Safan? The next time we're put together, I want you to dig this fucking thing out of my back."

There was a pause before he answered. "I can't. I looked at yours when you were asleep. It's adhered to your spine. That's probably why you can't use your psi abilities, because it has direct contact with your brain stem. If I try to remove it, it could cause permanent paralysis...or worse."

Or worse...like the total loss of her psi powers. For a psion, that would be tantamount to making her a mental vegetable.

She started to tell him she agreed with him when suddenly the lights around them brightened, and she heard a loud whirring sound. At the same time, she sensed she was being moved. There was a bump as the two cells met, and the walls between her and the Ellinod disappeared.

Maurra got to her feet and turned toward the ship's doorway as the rest of the walls became transparent. Already the Kronners were filing into the hold, and overhead the eyes of the video cameras glittered.

It was show time again. Rest time was over. Maurra was aware of the Ellinod coming up behind her as the familiar voice boomed, "Excellent performance yesterday, you two. Now it's time to give our audience a repeat performance. Except this time you must do it differently."

"Differently?" Safan gruffly asked. Maurra didn't have to look at the creature to know his anger was rising. She knew exactly how he felt.

The voice tsked at them. "You are neither stupid nor naïve. You know as well as I do that if I keep giving my customers the same thing over and over, the same position, the same everything, they're going to tire and cancel their subscription. And we can't have that, can we?"

"Why not?" Mara challenged, hoping to piss him off. She wasn't expecting to hear laughter in reply.

"Why not? Simple, my dear JoJo. If they cancel their subscription, I cancel you. Or at least your Ellinod lover. If you want to stay alive, and keep him alive, then you had better give me another damn good show."

"Who are you?" the Ellinod suddenly bellowed, but his question was ignored. Once the Kronners were inside the hold, all unneeded light was extinguished. At the four corners of the combined cell, the hovering vids took their places.

"It's show time, my friends." The voice started to laugh again, but was abruptly cut off when the connection was closed.

It was time to perform again, but this time the show would definitely be different. Maurra glanced up at the Ellinod. Oh yeah. This time they would obey, but not in the way their captor expected.

Chapter Ten
Refusal

Maurra stood with her hands perched on her hips, legs spread and feet firmly planted on the floor. Behind her, the Ellinod towered over her, his arms crossed over his barrel chest. Although naked and broken, they remained defiant and more than angry. Together they made an imposing looking couple.

Vol Brod stared at them from his monitor, a smile already stretching his face. It was good to see the fire inside of them still burned.

"Are they really going to defy you again? And you're going to let them?"

Trainer remained staring at the two people inside the cell. "Let them. The more anger and fire we get out of them, the better the show. And the better the show, the more subscribers." He swiveled around in his chair to face the Kronner leader. "Speaking of subscribers, how are our numbers?"

"Excellent. After last night, we added another sixteen billion subscribers to the 3-D feeds alone."

"Good." Vol Brod turned his attention back to the monitors. "Then let me do my job and stop questioning me. If you don't like the way I'm handling this, you're more than welcome to pay me my share and let me go my merry way, and you can assume the burden for yourself." Dropping his voice, he added, "As long as they continue to defy me and fight me, the money will continue pouring in. Remember that." He signaled for the Kronner leader to be silent and pressed the transmission button on the console.

"You're wasting my time and my customers' time. Plus, my patience is growing thin. Fuck the Ellinod, JoJo."

"I'd rather fuck you." The JoJo lifted her chin and stared directly into his personal feed. "Come down here and take me on. I dare you."

Vol Brod dismissed the Kronner leader with a wave of his hand. Once the little man was gone, he rubbed his chin. This was better than he had hoped for. The bitch still had a lot fight in her, and he bet the Ellinod did, too.

Good. Very good. Vol Brod chuckled. "As much as I would like to, and as tempting as your offer may be, I'm afraid I'm no match for the Ellinod's prowess."

"Aww. What's the matter? Afraid you don't size up?" A sarcastic smile traced her lips. "Didn't anyone ever tell you it's quality, not quantity?"

Vol Brod frowned. "Quit wasting time. Are you going to fuck or not?"

To his delight, the couple remained unmoving.

"Very well. Mincred, shoot the Ellinod."

At his command, more than a dozen Kronners raised their weapons and aimed at the cell. The prisoners' reactions were immediate. Not surprisingly, the JoJo placed herself in front of the Ellinod.

Vol Brod laughed. "Do you realize how ludicrous you look?" he asked, chuckling. "The Ellinod towers over you by at least a foot. The Kronners will have no difficulty hitting him."

"Let them try," the woman dared.

Vol Brod closed the feed and opened a secondary one. "Mincred. I want one gun to fire at the Ellinod, am I clear?"

"I read you."

"When I say fire, I want *one* gun to hit the Ellinod, understand? Have the other weapons fire over and around the cell, but I don't want to kill the Ellinod. Not yet."

"I understand," the Kronner leader responded.

Vol Brod nodded to himself and returned to the main transmission. On the monitor he could see the JoJo and Ellinod had not moved.

"Last warning, JoJo. Start fucking the Ellinod or else he's dead, and your next lover will be the Par Matta waiting in the next hold."

As glad as he was to see the JoJo continue to fight him, Vol Brod knew he could only let her defy him for so long. Otherwise his customers would become restless, and restless customers were non-returning customers. He gave her to the count of ten before hitting the transmission button.

"Fire."

More than a dozen weapons exploded in the hold, nearly blinding him in every monitor. When the light and noise died down, he was happy to see the Ellinod writhing on the cell floor. The JoJo scrambled on hands and knees over to him, and it was then Vol Brod realized that the Ellinod had shoved her out of the way at the last micro-second to keep her from being hit.

"Safan!" She threw herself on top of the Ellinod to check his injuries.

Vol Brod stared in surprise and delight. Safan? She called the Ellinod by name? "Good. Very good," he murmured. That the JoJo was willing to give her life for the creature was expected, as that was her job. But for the Ellinod to do the same told him that a bond of some sort was growing between them. It would be that bond Vol Brod knew he could exploit.

"That was a warning, JoJo. Next time I'll order all the Kronners to fire on the Ellinod, and we all know the creature will not survive a direct hit from every weapon."

The JoJo looked up from where she was kneeling over the alien to stare at the nearest camera and gave an angry snarl. "I don't know who you are or why you're doing this, but I promise I'm going to kill you, you snurg-sucking lurch worm! Do you hear me? I'm going to find you, and when I do, I'm going to kill you!"

"Wouldn't that be against your JoJo credo?" he taunted her.

"You have no idea how much I can make your life a living hell. Give me one minute alone with you, you sick Mogra—"

Vol Brod laughed loudly. "Enough threats, JoJo. Fuck the Ellinod and get it over with. Now."

He closed communications and sat back to watch the monitors. He knew that eventually she would try to save the Ellinod anymore pain, which meant the next step was up to her.

Oh, yes. She'd fuck the Ellinod because she knew she had no choice. But also because somehow, in some way, he could tell that something emotionally was developing between them. And for the JoJo, it was no longer becoming a matter of fulfilling her duties, but more of a matter of fulfilling something more personal, now that she had formed that emotional attachment to him. Whether it was a need or a want was inconsequential. The JoJo would try to find a way to keep herself and the Ellinod alive.

And if by some miracle she managed to escape, Vol Brod would just have to make sure she never got within psi distance of him.

Chapter Eleven
Comparison

"Safan! You stupid, stupid..."

Beneath her hands the Ellinod's body continued to jerk and spasm in the wake of the blast he'd taken. His skin had gone nearly white with shock, but he was alive, and for that Maurra was grateful. Either the Kronners had been ordered to dial down the strength of their weapons, or not all of the Kronners had aimed for her, because if Safan had been hit with everything as The Voice had threatened to, he would be dead.

"That was a warning, JoJo. Next time I'll order all the Kronners to fire on the Ellinod, and we all know the creature will not survive a direct hit from every weapon."

Maurra looked up from where she was kneeling over the alien to stare at the nearest camera and gave an angry snarl. "I don't know who you are or why you're doing this, but I promise I'm going to kill you, you snurg-sucking lurch worm! Do you hear me? I'm going
to find you, and when I do, I'm going to kill you!"

"Wouldn't that be against your JoJo credo?" The Voice taunted her.

Fuck the credo. If she had to give up her position as a JoJo to make sure The Voice got what he deserved for what he was putting her and the Ellinod through, she would not hesitate stepping down.

"You have no idea how much I can make your life a living hell. Give me one minute alone with you, you sick Mogra—"

The Voice laughed. "Enough threats, JoJo. Fuck the Ellinod and get it over with. Now. You have fifteen galactic minutes to get results." There was a click, and Maurra knew the line of communication had been closed.

The clock was ticking.

Maurra bent back over the Ellinod and tried to focus on his injuries. She never expected the creature to push her away in order to take the barrage. Why would he pull such a stunt? Didn't the idiot realize she could shield herse—

Maurra suddenly felt a cold chill go through her. *Oh, shit! Ohhhh, shit! So who's the stupid one now?*

She had forgotten again. She had totally forgotten that her psi powers were tied to her ability to protect herself, and that included the shield she could throw up to deflect nearly every weapon she encountered. But a lifetime of being able to do things a certain way because she had been born with her unique gifts had made her forget that certain natural laws applied and could not be ignored.

She was without her psi powers as surely as if they had been stripped of her, yet she still had them...to an extent. But if she tried to use them, the feedback she'd receive through the little translation device could kill her. The pain she'd received in the past had been enough to convince her of that. What she didn't know was whether or not the translator was actually meant to nullify her, or if the pain was because of negative feedback.

She continued to lie on top of the Ellinod, to keep him from hurting himself with all the thrashing his nervous system was putting him through. He was completely oblivious of the present. There was no telling how much pain he was having to endure.

Fortunately it wasn't long until she started to see some improvement. Gradually, the Ellinod's color returned and his body started to calm. His eyes rolled back down from their sockets until they were able to focus on her leaning over him. He frowned.

"Maurra?"

She reached over and slapped him hard on the cheek. "Don't you ever do that again, understand me?" she hissed at him. "You stupid humanoid. I meant to take those rays."

"They would have killed you!" Safan finally managed to rasp.

"Then they would have killed me! I'm a JoJo. Great gods, don't you think I've encountered my share of half-crazed lunatics with a thirst for vengeance before? Or have you forgotten it's my sworn duty to protect creatures like you? And for you to put yourself in danger by preventing me from doing my job is not only an insult to me and my profession, but...but..." She stopped and willed herself to calm down. She was overreacting, and they both knew it. But, hell, considering the circumstances...

He was trying to save your life, a little voice sarcastically reminded her.

"I couldn't let them kill you," Safan told her gruffly. If she didn't know better, he seemed disappointed. Apparently his attempt at self-sacrifice wasn't getting the kind of reaction he'd hoped for.

"Why not?" Maurra shot back. "We're only in this mess because Mr. Voice has it out for me. If the Kronners kill you, they'll bring in the Par Matta. After the Par Matta, heavens knows what other sick perversion they'll plan for me." She gave him another angry slap on the shoulder before swiping at her eyes with the back of her wrist. "But if I die, there won't be any reason for this travesty to go on. They'll let you go."

"You don't know that."

She shook her head. He was right. So far everything was still a guessing game.

"No, I don't know that, but do you think they'd draw many customers if one of the two people in this cell wasn't a JoJo?"

"I hate to break up this very interesting conversation, but our customers are getting impatient," The Voice interrupted with more than a hint of irritation. "Rationalization time is over. Get on with what people are paying good creds to see! You are now down to five galactic minutes."

Maurra raked her eyes over the naked Ellinod, resting briefly on the flaccid penis lying between his thighs. "How do you feel?"

"Like tiny Ludunol worms are crawling all over my body, inside and out, and leaving scorch marks where they pause to electrocute me," he admitted.

"Can you get it up?" Turning to look into his face, she noticed his gaze riveted on her mound and thighs. She glanced down to see what held his attention and saw the streaks of dried blood marking the insides and outsides of her legs.

"Can you take me again?" he countered.

"Ignore the blood. Most of that's from when you were holding me down last time with your damn claws. Come on. Tell me what to do. Do you want me on the bottom again? Can you manage it?"

"I'll need you on top," Safan said. "I haven't quite gotten full use yet of my body."

Maurra threw her leg over him and settled herself on top, sitting slightly back on top of his lap, with the creature's testicles and dick nestled in front of her and against her mound. "Tell me what feels good," she ordered him, taking his penis in her hands.

"Anything you do feels good," he admitted in a softer voice. "You're not much different from the females of my world, did you know that?"

"Really?" She was stroking him with both hands, pumping him vertically in front of her. Already she could tell he was responding. Behind them the vid cameras maneuvered around the corners to get a better shot of what was happening.

Safan laid his enormous hands on her knees. Maurra immediately knew he was trying to keep himself focused, as well as her, on their need to get this over with.

"You mean, not that much different in the way you make love to them, right?" she clarified.

He gave a single nod. "Our females have breasts and nipples, like you. They like to have them played with and suckled and massaged, like you do. And your clit is very responsive to stimulation."

"Well, your cock is very responsive to stimulation, too," she commented wryly. Already the erection was able to stand on its own, having filled out to an impressive size. Letting go with one hand, Maurra reached down to gently roll a sac in her palm. "Do you like me to touch your balls?"

His answer was barely a breath. "Yes."

For another minute or two she played with the Ellinod's nuts, holding the baby-soft orbs in the warmth of her palm and teasing them with gentle scrapes of her fingernails. In her other hand the erection stiffened until the veins along the sides stood out in relief, and the huge helmet-shaped head darkened with blood.

He had no hair on his body. None anywhere. It was natural for his species, yet it felt strange to experience a lover without any. As she ran her nails over the tender skin around the base of his genitals, she kept checking his facial expression to see how she was doing. He continued to watch her, but every now and then he closed his eyes to savor what he was feeling.

Leaning over, Maurra placed the erection between her breasts and folded herself around it. Slowly, she ran herself up and down the engorged dick, using the slight seepage from the end of the helmet to help lubricate. A deep, sensuous groan rumbled inside him.

There was a gentle nudge against her hips. The beast's large hands curved around her buttocks.

"Enough. Up."

His erection slid out from between her breasts as he lifted her to her knees. Grabbing himself with one hand, Safan placed himself between her thighs. Gently, the head of his dick rubbed her clit, massaging and titillating the stiff bud, tickling and preparing her. Immediately she felt herself responding. A familiar warmth coated her outer lips as seductive heat began building up within her.

"Ohhhh."

The oversized head slid to her entrance and started burrowing into her channel. Inch by inch it progressed, tunneling inside her as Maurra wriggled her hips to coax him further in. Safan tilted her a bit forward to make sure her clit remained in contact with his erection, keeping the desire sliding through her veins like thick spice.

Guilt raised its ugly head. She shouldn't be enjoying this. She shouldn't be reacting this way to what the Ellinod was doing to her, but she couldn't help herself.

Huge, burning hot, and un-fucking-believably thick, it stretched her, filled her, and almost threatened to rip her apart with its girth.

"Maurra, you feel..."

The earthquake trembled within her. It was growing steadily. Rising. Becoming stronger and more potent. Safan slid further inside. Once he was nearly halfway up inside her, he pumped her slightly, just enough to slather more of her juices around his tight skin to further ease his way. Another pump, and her body slipped to the edge of release. It teetered, almost there, almost crashing, almost toppling over into oblivion, when his dick began to quiver.

No. Vibrate.

Vibrate against her engorged clit. Against her inner walls where the least little movement was already sending her into orbit.

Maurra started to call out his name when her orgasm blasted through her. At the same time, Safan slammed himself up into her as far as he could go. Her inner walls contracted, strangling his cock, and he roared in pain and release.

* * *

Sitting in front of the vid monitors with his own dick in his hands, Tramer Vol Brod began laughing hysterically at the 3-D close-up of the Ellinod erupting inside the JoJo. Seconds later, he followed suit.

Life was good, he decided. Life was so good. This was the best revenge he had ever cooked up, and it was only the beginning for the JoJo. Only the beginning.

Smiling, he leaned back in his chair and closed his eyes, sated.

Chapter Twelve
Silence

The walls were opaque again. Somehow she knew it before she opened her eyes. But she didn't smell food like she had the last time she'd regained consciousness. Things were different.

Also unlike last time, she was warm. Not comfortable. Not when she was lying on a cold, unforgiving floor. But at least she wasn't shivering from the chill.

A movement at her back alerted her.

Safan.

She blinked, awakening further. Safan was still in the cell with her?

Slowly, Maurra rolled over to face the hulking beast. She gritted her teeth against the aches and sharp, stabbing pains she felt as she shifted her position. The creature was watching her with his green eyes. A worry line creased his brow, if that little pucker meant the same thing as it did on humans. "How much longer do you think we must endure this torment?" he whispered so softly, she could barely hear him.

Maurra started to answer him when a very ugly truth hit her. Torment. The beast considered having to screw her as a torment. She felt her soul shrivel into a tiny knot and sink to the bottom of her stomach. He considered it torment, but she...

Oh, gods. What's happened to me?

His question had hurt in a way she'd never expected it to. And the realization of what she was beginning to feel shocked her. The horrible part was, her reality was just the opposite, and acknowledging that much was beginning to terrify her.

When the Ellinod took her, it was one of the most incredible acts she had ever endured. No matter how much she wanted to deny it, no matter how much she tried to degrade the act and take it down to its worst consequence, at some point she had come to accept it. Worse, she had discovered she enjoyed being fucked by the Ellinod. She loved the way he was determined to see to her pleasure before he found his. What's more, she wanted him to do it again. And again.

But it can't be. This can't go on, she kept telling herself. First, she and the Ellinod had to get out of here. Next, they had to make the Kronners pay for their involvement. Following that, she had to make sure The Voice was suitably rewarded for everything she and Safan were forced to endure.

But the love making...

Curse her, but she knew she would never find another lover to satisfy her the way Safan did. Worse, she was developing feelings for him and he was just trying to keep her alive. Somehow he had managed to take hold of her heart and wrapped his big hands around it to protect it. His acts of selflessness were strange and surprising to her. Too bad they weren't being reciprocated.

Enough self-pity, Maurra. Get to the job.

Maurra pointed to her mouth, pointedly closed it, and shook her head. If they were going to plan a way out of this mess, it had to be done in complete silence as everything they said was being monitored.

Safan gave a slow nod. His eyes remained riveted on her face. He understood.

She pointed at the nearest wall, made the motion of a door opening with her hands, then fired a make-believe ray with her hand. The Ellinod gave another nod. Before the Kronners could fire on them, the walls of the cell had to be lowered first.

Teething her lower lip, Maurra knew this next bit would be harder to explain. She could only hope Safan would accept her idea.

She pointed to the wall again, then to herself, tapping her forehead, and made the motion of throwing her psi powers outward. The Ellinod stared at her in wide-eyed shock. Maurra placed a hand on his mouth to keep him from blurting out.

She repeated the throwing of her psi powers, then pantomimed becoming unconscious. Prodding his chest, she motioned lifting an object and pointed to herself. A raised eyebrow asked if he was following her.

He frowned but nodded. Yes, but he wasn't happy with her suggestion. He pushed her forehead with a thick finger and made a gesture like breaking a stick in half. Then he thumped her chest, curled his fingers into a fist that pulsed like a beating heart, and suddenly threw his hand open to simulate that heart exploding.

If she used her psi powers, it was almost certain it would kill her.

I know. She nodded as she hardened the expression on her face. *But it's my job. You have to accept that. It's part of the risk I take every day. But if my sacrifice frees you from this hellish nightmare...*

Maurra steeled herself. Now came the hard part. How to tell him to find the nearest life boat so they could make their escape.

Safan gently shook her shoulder. He knew that when she used her powers at full strength, it would permanently burn out every synaptic nerve in the Kronners' bodies, rendering them not only unconscious, but many if not all of them would become complete vegetables. But the toll on her...

The Ellinod pointed to himself and made a flying motion with his hands. She had to admit it was a pretty good imitation of a survival pod. Maurra nodded.

The cells began to move. A crack appeared in the floor and widened until the two holding areas separated. Safan grasped her tighter against him as he scooted away from the edge. The walls remained opaque, and for a few seconds Maurra could see the outside wall of the hold. A split second later, the missing wall appeared, leaving them together inside the smaller cell.

Maurra looked up at the beast, who gave her an equally puzzled stare. This was a new development, leaving them together.

They dragged themselves up to a sitting position when the opposite wall clarified. On the other side two Kronners stood, each holding a tray of food. Safan prodded her buttock, silently asking if they should use this opportunity to try to escape. Maurra reached back and grabbed his hand as she slowly shook her head.

No. Not now. Not yet, but soon.

They remained motionless at the far end of the cell as the Kronners cautiously approached with their food. Once they left the trays on the cell floor, the two little aliens hurried away, and the cell wall went white.

Immediately Safan shoved her around to face him. The expression on his face said it all. He was furious with her for not taking the chance when they had it. Maurra let him make his threatening gestures before taking his hands and holding them tightly to her chest.

Trust me, she mouthed silently. *Trust me.*

The Ellinod remained puzzled. He didn't know her language, no more than she knew his, but he must have recognized the pleading look on her face and in her eyes.

Sighing loudly, he detached himself from her and crawled over to the far end to fetch their trays.

They ate in silence. When they were finished, Safan threw the empty trays at the wall and reached for her. Maurra let him pull her roughly against him as he settled back down on the floor on his side. Stretching out a heavily-muscled arm, he guided her head down, urging her to use it as a pillow, and gently brushed her hair over her chest and belly for further warmth. With her buttocks nestled in his crotch, the Ellinod threw his other arm over her until she was safely ensconced in his embrace.

She was warm, she was fed, and she was oddly comfortable.

She was asleep within minutes.

Chapter Thirteen
Suspicion

"Why are you letting them stay together?" the Kronner leader asked.

"To strengthen their bond," Vol Brod replied with a grin. Seeing the little alien's surprised expression, he laughed. "Oh, come now, Mincred. Don't tell me you haven't noticed. Our JoJo and the Ellinod are developing a thing for each other. I want to exploit that. That way, when I finally separate them permanently, and force the Ellinod to watch her being fucked by another species, that show alone will bring in at least another two or three billion customers!"

Mincred laughed, a high-pitched giggle that had to be the most annoying sound in twelve galaxies. "You are good, Vol Brod! Your mind is twisted in ways we like. It was a good thing we became partners, don't you agree? So tell me, is that what's next on our plan? To bring in a new species for the JoJo?"

Turning his seat around, Vol Brod tapped the visual readout on the console. "We're nearing the Cojuanna Taburi system. There's a bar on the fourth moon of CT Four."

The Kronner nodded excitedly. "Brom Enni Taro. We know it well. There's a small settlement there, but the bar is the biggest draw. It's very popular with criminals and law breakers."

Criminals and law breakers? How apropo. Smiling, Vol Brod asked, "Think we can find a humanoid species there suitable for the JoJo?"

"I would bet my life on it!"

Good, because that's exactly the penalty you'll pay if you screw up, Vol Brod silently promised. He flashed another fake smile at the little alien. "Good! Tell your men to prepare. But remember, I must approve their selection before they bring it down, understand? I want to check it out to make sure it's in good health, and that it's something my viewers would want to see take on the JoJo."

"Don't worry," Mincred assured him. "My men are well trained." He glanced at the monitor showing the cell with its crystallized walls. "Is it safe to keep them out of sight? What if they're preparing a plan of attack?"

"Oh, they're preparing something," Vol Brod said. "That's dead certain. The JoJo is too intelligent and too driven not to try and conceive a way out. Same goes for the Ellinod. But they also know that anything they say will be overheard, and I have the computers on the alert to let me know if they recognize any of the tags I've programmed into them."

"Tags?"

"Clue sounds. Certain words that would raise a red flag."

"What happens if the computer goes on the alert?" Mincred asked.

Vol Brod grinned broadly. "That would depend on what triggered the alarm," he said. Glancing back at the first monitor, he added, "Get the shuttle prepared. We should reach CT Four in less than a galactic hour."

The Kronner leader hurried away without an acknowledgment, but it didn't matter. Once the little alien was gone, Vol Brod turned up the volume in the hold in case the two captives said anything.

What the Kronners didn't know about was that all it would take from him was one word, and the entire ship would explode. They would never reach Kronnaria. The little aliens would never see their home world again. The JoJo and her new Ellinod lover would vanish. Better yet, all trace of the video setup would disappear, becoming mere atoms in the void of space. There would be no proof left of his involvement, and therefore no way he could be held accountable for their deaths and destruction. But before that happened, he would be inside his little escape pod and a safe distance from the detonation.

A quick check of his bank accounts verified the wealth he was accumulating. Thus far he had over two dozen accounts spread throughout thirteen solar systems. Each account was under a different name and separate I.D., and he was the only one who knew the keywords and combinations to release the funds.

He checked the tiny mark inside his wrist. A chip no bigger than a grain of sand was embedded beneath his epidermis. All the information and verification he would need to withdraw his monies when he needed them was locked inside it.

A light went off near his elbow. *Hello. Speaking of the devil. It looks like it's time to open another one.*

Once an account reached a certain limit, the computer would notify him so he could open a new one, since an unusually large balance on a relatively new account would raise a red flag. No sense alerting the authorities when it could be avoided.

New account, new name, new way to elude detection in order to keep what he'd worked so hard for. That way if one account was discovered or the funds were nullified, he had the others to fall back on. After initiating a fresh location for his holdings, it was a simple matter to point his portion of the initial funds flowing directly into the Kronners' account toward it, making the whole process better than siphoning. In fact, the Kronners were the ones in control of how many creds he was to receive of each paid subscription. They were so focused on the numbers, they never paid attention to what Vol Brod did with his percentage. Besides, where he put his stash was none of their business.

A small moan caught his attention. Vol Brod turned to the monitor overlooking the cell. It took a bit of self-control not to clarify the cell walls so he could see what the two prisoners were up to. As much as he hated to admit it, he'd gotten hooked on watching the couple perform. In some perverse way, he got off on it.

"Approaching Cojuanna Taburi system," the computer announced. "Initiating standard orbit around the fourth planet as programmed."

Within the hour the Kronners would be inside that little bar, searching for another likely candidate he would first have to approve. Once they did and had it aboard, they would resume heading for Kronnaria.

Except this ship would never make it.

Approximately six hundred thousand spacial miles lay between Cojuanna Taburi and Kronnaria. Vol Brod estimated there was enough time left for two more shows. Or, with luck, maybe three. He had been entertaining the thought of having his customers suggest another method of debasement. Something so degrading, it would remain in the minds of his subscribers for years. *Maybe I could put up a list of possibilities and let them vote.* There were so many to choose from. Bondage was always a favorite. As long as it dished out a lot of humiliation, he would be happy to consider it. Personally, he would love to see the JoJo suck the Ellinod's dick down her throat. Of course, the customers wouldn't be notified. No sense in signaling to everyone what was next on the agenda, or that everything would soon be coming to an end, because then he'd have to come up with some plausible explanation to suit the Kronners.

For certain there would be two more shows, and two more chances to fill the coffers. One of those shows would definitely be the separation of the JoJo and Ellinod, and watching the couple's reactions when the new species was introduced. As for the other show...

He rubbed his cheek and smiled. He'd always heard about the nearly bestial way an Ellinod took its mate. Now he had the chance to find out if it was as entertaining and degrading as it sounded.

That's what I'll do. I'll make him take her Ellinod style, and save introducing the new species for the final act. Once that's accomplished, I'm out of here, and the Kronners can kiss my rich ass goodbye. That is, if they have anything left to kiss with once I order the ship to blow itself up.

Vol Brod laughed. Having a plan thought out to the end was always a good thing because that meant it was as good as done.

Chapter Fourteen
Escape

He rubbed her back, concentrating on her shoulders as his huge hands worked the steel-hard knots into a more rubbery consistency. He brushed her long hair out of the way and targeted one particularly stubborn cluster. Maurra moaned. She'd never had a massage like this, where every sore spot was soothed, every tension-filled muscle eased. She wanted to ask him if this was another method of foreplay, or if he was doing it just because he wanted to.

At the thought of foreplay, she felt her vaginal muscles contract. Without a doubt she knew she was already creaming as her body prepared herself for another session. Prepared herself for him. Growing desire melted away the last shreds of sleep, and she bent forward slightly to give him easier access.

Something warm and hard nudged her buttocks. She wriggled her hips slightly, and the head of his erection slipped between them. Lifting one leg slightly enabled the head to dip past her anus until it rested against her clit. Maurra shifted herself and reached down between her thighs to touch the erection. The helmet head trembled when she ran her short nails over it.

Safan vibrated his erection. Not long, not hard, but it was enough to make her catch her breath and press her lips together to keep from making another sound. If the Kronners knew what was going on inside the cell...

What would they do? the little voice asked her with more irritation than curiosity. *Isn't this what they were wanting you to do anyway?*

Yes, but at their *discretion.*

Maurra mentally groaned. Listen to her. She was actually concerned about what the Kronners thought? About what *they* wanted?

What hell is wrong with me?

It was one of the first signs she was starting to break.

A shudder interrupted any further thought. He was teasing her, easing his erection to her entrance, pressing the head almost all the way into her, then withdrawing. Coating her inner lips and thighs with her hot juices. He pushed into her again another inch...and remained there. Maurra started to glance over her shoulder at him when a warm, heavy breath blew over her skin. Slowly, Safan removed his erection, leaving her feeling strangely incomplete.

She looked back at him, but he refused to meet her stare. Maurra started to sit up when a movement at the corner of her eye caught her attention. The walls of the cells turned glassy, and like all the other times, she could see Kronners lining the outer circumference of the hold, standing just outside of vid range. Because she couldn't use her psi powers to automatically realize the exact number, Maurra began counting. She'd hit twenty when The Voice came from overhead.

"I hope you enjoyed your meal and nap."

Maurra gave the ceiling a dirty look but refused to answer. Neither did she nor the Ellinod stand up, but remained seated.

"Ellinod! You are a very fine specimen for your race, do you know that? I've also heard some very interesting stories about the way Ellinod males mate with their preferred females. Very...exciting...stories. So I've decided to make that your next challenge. Are you listening, Ellinod? I order you to take the JoJo and fuck her as if she's your preferred mate."

To Maurra's surprise, Safan jumped to his feet, his massive hands curled into fists. "You cannot force mates!" the Ellinod snarled loudly. "You cannot force me to take the JoJo if she isn't ready, and I cannot take her as a mate if we are not bonded!"

A moment of silence stretched into two. "Sooo...am I to assume you're refusing to obey my command?" The Voice was soft and undeniably threatening.

Getting to her feet, Maurra countered, "You heard him, you Kronner ass licker. I'm not his mate, so therefore he can't take me in that manner you've got a hard-on to watch."

This was it. She had thrown down the challenge. Although she and Safan knew what most likely would happen next, they had to be prepared for it. Maurra could feel her psi powers taking notice. Carefully, she kept them covered and in the dark. Otherwise the telltale sparkle at her forehead would be a dead giveaway to the Kronners. That, and her reaction to the unimaginable pain that would follow soon after.

The Voice laughed. "When are you going to learn it's futile to deny me? To be brutally honest, I'm getting tired of this. I'm not going to banter back and forth anymore with you. If that's your final word—"

"This is coming to a halt. All of it. Right now," she told him with as much finality as she could muster.

"Mincred!"

A Kronner at the end of the line came to sudden attention. "Yes, Vol Brod!"

Maurra's breath caught in her throat. At the same time, a deep heat flushed her face. "Vol Brod?" She made eye contact with the lens of the closest vid camera and refused to turn away. "Tramer Vol Brod? Listen to me, Vol Brod. We're not doing your sick bidding any longer. And now that I know you're the evil fuck behind all this, I am officially putting a bounty on your head," she informed him with a small smile.

"Go ahead and try, JoJo. You're still my prisoner, and your next lover won't need me to order him to fuck you. Mincred, kill the Ellinod! *Now!*"

The Kronner paused, his face pale at the unexpected order. Maurra could immediately see this part of the show had not been planned or rehearsed. When the alien set his neuron ray where it reflected a black light, she knew Safan was seconds away from death.

"*I said now, you worthless piece of kruart shit!*" Vol Brod screamed.

Nervously, the leader advanced toward the cell and pointed his gun directly at the Ellinod's head. He'd moved closer to make certain he'd hit the huge beast and not her. Maurra took a step sideways, putting herself directly in front of Safan. It was a futile gesture since the beast towered behind her, but she didn't do it as much to protect him as she did to give herself unrestricted access to the others in the hold.

"Good try, Maurra," Vol Brod chuckled, using her real name for the first time. "Say goodbye to your lover."

Behind her she could tell the Ellinod was steeling himself. She could almost sense his fear for her, as much as she could sense him wishing her luck.

Two one-hundredths of a second. That's all I need. Less than two one-hundredths of a second.

She would not know the Kronners had dropped the invisible wall until Mincred fired. That meant she had to second-guess the alien. In two one-hundredths of a second, she could fire her powers. Maurra prayed she was accurate, that she'd survive, and that both she and Safan would be able to escape. Otherwise...

She saw the barely perceptible movement of the Kronner's hand on the weapon. With a snarl, she opened herself up, letting her considerable psionic powers blaze through every cell in her body as she directed them forward in one final explosion of energy. The agony that tore through her brain seized every organ in her body and stopped her heart.

Time and the present ceased to be.

Chapter Fifteen
Ellinod

Consciousness.

Aware, but barely.

She was free floating. Weightless. Warm.

She couldn't move. Her hands wouldn't obey. Neither would her legs. Or her eyes. She was breathing, but beyond that nothing else existed. Everything was black. Still. Quiet. Or maybe her ears had stopped working, too.

What...

Where...

Blank. Silence except for the sound of her lungs taking in air. Working automatically. She could hear.

She was breathing. Or maybe something was breathing for her. It was hard to tell.

The pain was gone, but the damage remained. She couldn't think. It was impossible to think, so she chose not to.

It was easier to slide back into the comforting blackness.

* * *

Voices. More than one. She couldn't identify them. It hurt too much to try, but she could hear them. Hear what they were saying.

"I don't have that kind of facility or the training, Orgoran. I wish I did. Gods in the heavens, I wish I did."

"She's dying. Her brain is shutting down sections at a time. Isn't there something you can do?"

That last voice was familiar. It sounded like soft gravel.

"I can put her in a stasis tube. It will at least help keep her body alive until you can find help."

"I'll be forever grateful. Anything else?"

"There are a couple of facilities with excellent mental clinics. You're in luck. The closest is on Kronnaria."

"I can't take her there. The Kronners are not above killing her if they find out she's a JoJo. Is there anyone else? Any place closer?"

"All I can suggest is that you go to Ellinod. It's the only other nearest planet I know of that can handle her type of care."

Go to Ellinod. That name was familiar, but it floated just beyond her reach, ghostly and indistinct.

It hurt to listen. It hurt more to try to understand.

She slept.

* * *

"Maurra."

A voice. Gentle. Soft, like rain on rocks.

"Maurra?"

She opened her eyes. There was a light. Diffused. Greenish. Unfocused and hazy.

"Maurra, if you can hear me, just listen. Don't think, just listen. You're alive. We're safe. The Kronners are dead. I'm taking you back to Ellinod. It's the closest planet with a medical facility that can help you."

Her body no longer belonged to her. It was detached, or her brain was. She didn't want to think, but something sat beyond her vision. Something she couldn't identify. When she tried, nothing happened. She breathed. Her heart beat. She was alive. It was enough.

"Maurra, when we get there I'll have the physicians remove the translation device."

Translation device. The words held no meaning. There was now, but that was all she could grasp. Everything else remained *out there*, beyond her grasp and understanding.

"Maurra, I owe you my life. But I owe you more. Much more."

A hand came into view on the other side of the fuzzy green stuff. A large hand. Five digits. Humanoid. It moved in front of her like it was waving. Maurra watched its slow movement.

"Sleep, Maurra. Go back to sleep. Hopefully the next time you awaken, you'll be on your way to recovery."

Go back to sleep. The voice told her to sleep.

She closed her eyes.

* * *

A smell. A scent. Unrecognizable.

And she felt heavy. Restricted.

A sound. A movement.

Opening her eyelids was almost too difficult to do, but she managed to open them to find herself in an enclosed space. A room, not a cell. A cell didn't have a bed or giant pillows on the floor. The tug of gravity on her body told her she was no longer free floating.

Planetside. Or moonside. Some place strange. Some place she didn't remember.

The movement came again. It was beside her. Maurra tried to turn her head but it refused to budge. Neither would her eyes swing to the side to look. Gods, she was so tired. So unbelievably tired.

Giving up, she closed her eyes.

* * *

"Maurra."

The voice was soft and unfamiliar. She waited.

"Maurra, you need to dream. You need to start dreaming again. Your brain has been dormant too long. It's not keeping your body alive. Dream, Maurra. Go back to a place where you were happy. Where you were content. Or try to recall an event in your life you've never forgotten. Remember it. Recall it. Relive it."

Dream. Recall. Remember. Relive.

Like the time when she was three, and her mother and father were going...somewhere. In a ship. Going somewhere on...a holiday. A vacation. They were leaving their planet and heading out into space, but a piece of debris came from out of nowhere and slammed into the hull, right above the front viewscreen. There was screaming and an explosion. She had thrown up her hands as she cried out, and she'd felt a tingling itch latch on above her eyes. Tickling her skin. When she'd opened her eyes to look at what had happened, her part of the ship was still intact. The rear of the ship remained, although it was open now to space and everything was cartwheeling out of control. Terrified, she'd kept her hands up. Somehow she knew that by doing so she'd remain enclosed inside that pale pinkish bubble that was keeping her alive. Inside whatever was creating it.

Fortunately, a nearby ship had witnessed the collision, and they sent a team over to see if there were any survivors. She remembered how one woman stared at her in disbelief. Reflected in the woman's helmet visor, Maurra could see herself encased within that pale pinkish bubble that sizzled when the woman approached.

It was the first time she had ever used her psi powers.

It was the first time she discovered her destiny.

* * *

"Maurra, wake up. Maurra?"

Consciousness softly landed on its feet. Maurra took a deep breath. *I'm still alive? Amazing.*

"Maurra, I know you can hear me. You need to wake up now."

Gradually, she tried to crack open her eyelids but the damn things were caked, sealed shut. Reflex made her reach up and try to rub them open with her hands.

Someone took her hand and gently pulled it away. A warm, wet something proceeded to clean her eyes for her.

"There. Now try."

This time she had no difficulty. Maurra opened her eyes to see an immense creature hovering over her. A beast-like alien that resembled...

"Are you an Ellinod?"

The creature snorted and pulled back. "Welcome back to the land of the living, JoJo. How do you feel?"

She didn't have to think twice to answer the question. "Like melting shit. Where am I?"

"You're on Ellinod, in one of our best hospitals," the beast replied. It turned and walked away. Maurra tried to follow it as far as her restricted line of sight would let her.

She was lying down on a bed of sorts. A thin, silvery sheet or blanket covered her from the chest down. The room was lit with a low-level radiance. There was no way to tell if it was night or day, or how long she had been here.

"Did you save my life?"

"No," the voice answered from somewhere nearby. "I'm only a physician. I and several others have worked very hard to bring your mind back online. Once we accomplished that, your body healed itself." The Ellinod reappeared, this time with what looked like a bag filled with a purplish fluid. The bag also had a spout. "Are you thirsty?"

At the mention of thirst, Maurra felt her throat tighten up and her tongue swell. She nodded, and the physician placed the spout between her lips. The cool, slightly tangy liquid gushed into her mouth, immediately giving her some clarity. She drank until the bag was empty, then watched as the Ellinod backed away.

"Are you male? You sound male, but you don't look it." The question blurted out of her before she could think about it. Under normal circumstances, her examination would have been a terrible breach of etiquette. Maurra hoped the creature would understand and forgive her. To her surprise, the Ellinod smiled.

"Yes, I am a male. My name is Votul."

"Where are your horns?"

The beast turned his back on her, but she could still hear his answer. "Only the Orgoran have the privilege of keeping their horns."

"The what? Orgoran? What's an Orgoran?"

A yawn interrupted any further questions. She realized there had been a sleeping agent in the drink.

The physician turned around to face her as her mind started to go fuzzy on her. "An Orgoran is a Law Keeper like you, except he doesn't have any powers other than his training and skills."

A Law Keeper. The Ellinod police. A vague memory told her they were judge and jury all rolled into one. Like her, they had the right to detain and punish. Unlike her, they also had the right to obliterate.

Maurra wanted to know more, but the drug was quickly shutting down this brief moment of reality. Determined, her last mental thought was one word, one vision, that she grasped so tightly it would be the first thing she would remember when she woke up.

Safan.

Chapter Sixteen
Revived

Safan.

Safan.

He stood a few feet away looking strong and powerful. Green eyes bored into her, searching for proof that she was recovering. Needing a sign that her psyche was restored. Searching for Maurra.

"Safan."

His face went gray. "Maurra, how do you feel?"

Mentally or physically? Physically she felt stronger. Mentally...

Maurra took a deep breath and opened her eyes to find two Ellinod staring at her from the foot of the bed. Both looked like strangers, as far as she could tell. And since neither creature had horns, she was at a loss as to whether they were male or female.

Did it really matter?

"Safan?"

"You've been dreaming," one of them told her.

"What's the verdict?" she asked. Her throat felt scratchy, but she was afraid if she asked for something to drink, it would be spiked like the last time.

"We want to run a few more tests to make sure your recovery is sufficient to allow us to release you," the one on the right said.

Sweet planets, they even sounded like physicians. It was wonderful, but something was...off. She couldn't put her finger on what was different, but—

They sounded? As her memory returned, she shot a hand to her back and gave them a wide-eyed, questioning stare. The Ellinod on the left gave a slow nod.

"We were able to remove the translation device. Unfortunately, you'll bear a scar there for the rest of your life. We apologize."

That explained what had alerted her. It was the removal that was different. The tingling sensation to warn her was gone. The lack almost left her lightheaded. "It's all right," she told them. "You got the fucking...excuse me. You got it out of me. Is there any residual damage as a result?"

"That's what we were hoping you would tell us," the physician on the right replied and gestured toward the wall beside her. "Can you focus your powers on the wall?"

Maurra turned her head and concentrated. Something licked her forehead like a sweet treat. A warm sun burst into existence inside her head. In the next second scarlet light washed over the stone wall.

"And not a smidge of pain," Maurra grinned. Oh, dearest heavens, it felt wonderful! She looked back at the two physicians. "I'm cured!"

"Well, not exactly," the physician to her left said. "You're still weak. Another day or two of solid bed rest, and you'll be free to go. But you'll need at least another week before reporting back to duty."

Something nudged her memory, which was slowly coming back to her.

"Wait. If you took the translation device off me, how am I able to understand you?"

"By the I.D. strip on your arm," the left physician indicated.

It was then she noticed the tiny, almost jewel-like sparkle on top of her wrist, next to the bone. "There's a translator inside?" Instead of the low echo of their voices below the digital broadcast in her brain, like there had been with the Kronners' device, there was now an almost fluid translation that seemed to emerge directly from their mouths. The difference was phenomenal.

"If the Kronners had placed the device anywhere else on you other than your spine, we believe you would not have been barred from using your powers," the left physician added.

"But we have every reason to believe that's exactly where they had intended to put it," Right Physician said. Giving a little shrug of his/her massive shoulders, he/she continued. "The device was designed to plug directly into the synaptic nerve endings in your brain. It's very possible they knew exactly what kind of reaction it would cause if you tried to use your psi powers after it was integrated."

Maurra caught the fact that the physicians had mentioned the Kronners, which meant they must know the story of what had happened to her and Safan. A cold wind blew through her. That might explain why the Ellinods were keeping their distance from her. At first she had thought they were acting a bit standoffish because they knew she was a JoJo. It was a typical reaction from civilians, and one she was accustomed to.

Unfortunately, these last few days as a prisoner of the Kronners was a whole different matter. A very serious matter. She felt the smile slide off her face. Had they seen any of the vids?

"Where's Safan?"

From their body posture, she could tell they had immediately gone on the defensive. "That's restricted information," Right Physician finally told her.

"I'm a JoJo. Ellinod is within my jurisdiction. If you won't tell me, I can hold you in contempt," Maurra softly threatened. She hated to pull rank on them, especially after all they had done to save her life, but she owed her life to Safan, too. "I want to thank him for saving me. It's the least I can do before I leave here. Please tell me how I can see him."

Strange, how the lie tripped off her tongue as though it was the actual truth. Well, some of it was. She did want to thank him for saving her life. But more than that, she wanted to have an honest and open, non-restricted conversation with him about what had happened. Just her and him.

And then...maybe afterwards...they might...

She gripped the blanket covering her. Across the room the two physicians glanced at each other. Almost a full minute passed before Left Physician said, "We will let the Neris Orgoran know your request. It will be his decision whether or not to let you see him."

Maurra felt a frown knit her brows. "Neris Orgoran. I take it he's the head of everything?"

Left Physician nodded as the Right Physician said, "You need to eat. We need to get you off intravenous feeding and get some real nourishment into your body. We'll have a tray delivered if you feel you can handle it."

At the mention of food, the vision of a brown, lumpy substance flashed into her mind's eye. There was no telling what the Ellinods would send for her to eat, but anything had to be better than the tasteless crap the Kronners had forced her to eat.

Maurra forced a small smile. "Thank you. I didn't realize how hungry I was until you mentioned food. Can I have some water first before you go?"

Right Physician left the room, leaving Left Physician to bring her a carafe from a small alcove in the wall that she hadn't known existed. A small table appeared by her side, and the Ellinod set the carafe there.

"If you need us for anything, speak into the translator and an assistant will notify us."

The physician gave her a slight nod and left the room. Maurra counted to ten, then raised the translator strip to her lips.

"I'd appreciate it if you'd bring me something I can wear. It can be anything, but if you want me to get my strength back, I need to exercise. Like maybe take a few laps around the hospital. But before I can do that, I need some clothes."

She waited to hear a response, but she heard nothing. Not from the room or from the strip.

Now that she had a moment to herself, she closed her eyes and cleared her mind. Once her psyche was calm, she sent a mental probe through her body, looking for internal wounds or injuries. Looking for… She took a deep breath. Her womb was clean. She wasn't pregnant. Relief was sweet.

Crossing her arms over her chest, Maurra waited to see what would happen next, placing bets on whether she'd see her dinner, some clothes, or the Neris Orgoran.

Right now the odds were even, but her newly revived psionic powers were starting to lean toward the Neris. Some things never changed, no matter what planet or solar system she was in, and one of them was that administration always cut to the front of the line.

Chapter Seventeen
Unclean

She lost her bet. Or maybe it was because of proximity that her food arrived moments before there came a loud knock on her hospital door. Maurra gave the stuff in the bowl another dubious look. "Come in! I'm awake!"

The Ellinod that strolled in radiated arrogance, elitism, and disdain. Maurra immediately went on guard. At first glance he could have been Safan's twin, except for the slightly longer horns and the dark eyes. She recognized the uniform as being the same one Safan had been wearing when the Kronners attacked him. Maurra pointed to the contents of the bowl sitting in front of her. "Please tell me what this is."

The Neris Orgoran raised an eyebrow in surprise but tilted his head slightly and looked at the contents. "It's joolis."

"Is that vegetable or animal matter?"

"It's derived from the jajool plant. It's quite good."

"All right. I'll take your word for it," Maurra said, digging in with her two-tined utensil. She shoved some of the blue-green stuff into her mouth and paused to let her taste buds vote. *Give the Neris food critic a pat on the back.* "You're right. It's tasty. Sooo, I take it you're the Neris Orgoran?"

The Ellinod resumed his stance. "I'm here strictly as a courtesy, Joramansu."

Maurra continued to plow into her bowl of joolis, but she remained acutely aware of everything the Ellinod did or said, including the fact that he used her official calling and status. Or thought he did. She quickly deduced that the beast intended to follow the letter of the law by obeying rank. If that was the way he wanted to play, so be it.

"I'm not a Joramansu, Neris. I'm a Jurasu Roja. That trumps your Orgoran."

The Ellinod's eyes widened at her announcement. For a moment she got a whiff of the beast's shock. She also sensed his commitment to his job, and she reluctantly gave the creature credit for his unwavering loyalty. However, she was also sensing something else. Something diseased. Something dirty. No, not dirty. Stained. Permanently stained and beyond redemption.

She finished eating and set the bowl to the side. Her stomach felt stretched but content. No sign of rejecting her meal. Her strength was rapidly coming back. She just had to make sure she didn't push herself too much too soon, or else her recovery would take longer.

Might as well get to the bone of the matter. "I want to see Safan."

From the black scowl reappearing on the Neris's face, she could tell he was prepared for this argument. What the poor fool didn't realize was that she would eventually win. She always won.

"The Orgoran is currently awaiting sentencing, and is not allowed visitors."

"He's awaiting what? Why not?"

A tiny smile came over the beast's face at her surprise. "Safan broke Law Thirteen. As punishment, his title has been stripped of him, and he's awaiting word of further punishment."

"What's Law Thirteen?" Maurra demanded. As soon as she asked, she knew, and the memory of those days in the Kronner cell came back to her more vivid than ever.

"Fornication with another species."

"We were prisoners!" she almost yelled at him. Almost. At the last second, she sat up in bed and glared at him. "Our lives were at stake. We were punished if we refused. Didn't you see the vids?"

She watched in silent glee as the creature's face went a pasty gray. Apparently he had. She wondered if the Ellinod had been a subscriber, or if Vol Brod had deliberately beamed a feed to the planet just for the purpose of degrading Safan.

For that matter, did Vol Brod beam one to Headquarters, too?

Vol Brod. Maurra couldn't think about him now, so she tucked him into a mental pocket and continued to press the Neris. "What would you have done in that instance?"

"He should have refused."

"He did refuse! And he nearly died."

"Then he would have died," the Neris flatly stated.

Maurra gave the beast an incredulous look as another sensation of something impure wafted over to her. A spark went off in her head when it suddenly clarified. The Ellinod was thinking of her. Of her and Safan. They were now considered the unclean ones, no longer fit to mingle with the rest of humanity. Because of what they'd done, of what they'd been forced to do, they had become pariahs.

"Wait a minute! Our credo is to *save* lives, not take them! Yes, I know that my job obligates me to sacrifice myself to save others if there's no other solution, but you can't tell me that he should have let himself be killed over a simple fuck!"

The Neris's face went a shade paler but he remained resolute. "The law states—"

"What?" Maurra interrupted. "That law says what? That you kill yourself before you fuck another species?"

"You don't understand our ways," the beast growled.

"Apparently your ways have no regard for the sanctity of life," she shot back.

The Neris turned and started to depart. He was silently declaring an end to the conversation, but Maurra wasn't ready for him to go. Not yet.

"I demand to see Safan, and I demand the opportunity to approach those who would pronounce judgment on him so I can tell my side of the story."

The Ellinod paused near the doorway and glanced back at her, waiting.

"By my right as an interstellar council, and by right of the treaty which recognizes my status as a Jurasu Roja, I so will it, and you must obey," she further ordered. She saw the beast's eyes quickly look upward, then back down to her face. Maurra realized then that her psi powers had begun to glow. As her strength returned, so did her abilities. "If you have doubt as to my authority, you can contact—"

"I do not question your status, Jurasu," the Neris ceded. "I will inform the Tribunal of your request." Giving her a deferential nod, he left.

Seconds passed as Maurra calmed herself and soothed her power back into invisibility. She hadn't realized how worked up she'd become until she opened her fists to release her grip on the blanket. She'd won this battle. At least for now. Whether or not she would manage to get through to the Tribunal still hung in the air.

One thing, however, was very certain. By breaking the laws he'd sworn to uphold, there would be no leeway for Safan. No mercy. No quarter. He would be punished. How they would punish him remained to be seen. All she could hope for was that he'd be allowed to live. If he was allowed to live, then her own sacrifice would be worth it.

A wave of weariness swept over her, and Maurra laid back down to rest. She mustn't push it. *Conserve your strength, girl. Rest. The next battle will be here before you know it.*

It was good advice, but it wouldn't keep her from worrying about him.

Chapter Eighteen
Rejuvenation

The next time she awoke, Maurra found a pile of clothing sitting at the foot of the bed. Moving slowly, she managed to swing her legs over the side and scoot forward until her feet were flat on the cold floor. The wave of dizziness she'd expected never came. "So far, so good," she murmured. Standing up, however, was another problem. Her legs would not support her, and she fell back onto the bed. "All right. I take it back. This won't do, body. Time for a little rejuvenation."

She hadn't used her powers to revive herself since she'd mentally tried to fry herself and the Kronners. Closing her eyes, Maurra reached inside her psychic core. Her psi energy greeted her with the bounding enthusiasm of a loving pet. It was ready to be released, and more than eager to help.

The power surged through her body with the force of a tidal wave crashing onto a beach. Maurra gasped from the intensity as she fell across the bed, unable to move, unable to think. Unable to do anything until the power receded back into the center of her being where it awaited her next command. As it drained away, she could feel her toes and fingertips tingling. Her head felt clearer, her vision brightened, and even the aftertaste of the joolis teased her tongue.

Slowly, she sat up. "Let's try this again, shall we?"

On her second try, her legs remained strong, her balance unwavering. She grabbed the clothes to discover they were the simple drab brown pants and top worn by the average Ellinod. They were a bit too big for her, but that couldn't be helped. At least they provided her with some modesty. She ripped a piece of cloth from the bottom of one her pants legs and used it to tie back her hair.

"All right. If the moon won't come to the planet, let's see if the planet can go to the star."

She expected resistance, but no one tried to stop her as she walked out of her room and down the corridor. There was a small hub located at the end of the hallway. Two Ellinods looked up from where they stood behind a counter and blanched when they saw her. Their eyes remained locked on the gyrating sparkle sitting in the middle of her forehead.

"Where do you hold your prisoners?" Maurra asked politely, as if it was something every patient asked at some point during their stay.

One beast finally managed to stammer, "Th-there's a guard at the main doors. H-he can show you."

Maurra thanked them and followed the path pointed out to her. The other Ellinods who passed her gave her a wide berth, or ducked into doorways until she'd passed. But none of them challenged her.

The uniformed guard outside was expecting her. Maurra assumed he'd been notified by the terrified beasts at the counter. "Take me to see Safan," she ordered without any further explanation. By now it would be safe to bet that all of the planet was aware of Safan's transgression, just as they also knew who and what she was.

Nodding, the Ellinod spoke into his cuff. "This is Abrin. Leaving my post to escort the JoJo to the Consulate." Without waiting for a reply, the beast gestured for her to follow him.

She had never been on Ellinod before. After having dealt with only two or three of the beasts in the past, she had formed her own opinion about the species without any further investigation. But now, after the hours she had spent with Safan, and her visit to the planet, she was stunned to discover how misguided her original conceptions had been.

These people weren't only miners and jewelers. Their buildings were also carved monuments of beauty, sculpted out of enormous slabs of stone. Everywhere she turned, statues and life-size figures graced doorways and facades. The ground was set with glowing gemstones, and along the high borders surrounding each building, polished rocks gleamed with dark, intense color.

They passed a fountain decorated with rock creatures pouring water from various orifices. Maurra wondered if the fountains had any practical purpose other than ornamental until one Ellinod, towing a smaller version of itself, stopped, and the couple bent over to drink from the streams.

As she expected, those who spotted her became instantly wary and shied clear of her. Even the guard struggled to maintain a discreet distance away from her.

Overhead, Elto Norod, a medium-sized yellow sun, blazed midway between the horizon and directly overhead. Not too far away, she caught a glimpse of one of the planet's several moons, still visible and enormous due to its proximity, despite the sunlight. The air was still, the temperature pleasant. If it weren't for the circumstances she needed to tend to, Ellinod would have been a very nice place to spend some time.

The stones beneath her bare feet were worn smooth. Smooth and warm, and fit so perfectly together that there was no need for mortar. The more she observed, the more she realized little details about the place. Like the fact that this place was immaculate. There wasn't even a pebble or chunk of rock out of place for her to cut her feet on.

The Consulate was a monument of deep green stone. The moment they walked inside the open archway, the temperature dropped several degrees. Maurra wondered if this city remained temperate all the time. They came to another counter where an Ellinod in a different uniform greeted them.

"The JoJo is here," her guard announced. Nothing else. Not her intent, or even her name.

The other beast nodded and turned to her. "Follow me."

The guard remained behind while the guide led her further into the maze-like interior of the Consulate. The corridors were well-lit, although Maurra was at a loss to explain how.

They reached another carved door that, at first, looked like every other door they had passed, until she noticed the shiny black stone sitting next to the frame. The guide picked it up and placed it into a slot in the door. In response, the door ponderously swung inward. Pressing his hand on the stone, the guide looked at Maurra.

"When you are ready to come out, touch the key on the other side. If you call out, we won't be able to hear you."

Maurra nodded and walked into the dark hallway. Behind her, the guide removed the stone from its inset, and the door closed with a heavy, muffled thump.

Chapter Nineteen
Condemned

She got the impression this section of the Consulate was not for violent criminals. Maurra passed one empty holding area, then another, before she reached the one containing Safan. It looked less like a cell and more like someone had crudely dug a portion out of the rock. Pulse poles were embedded on either side of the wide doorway. Eyeing the shimmering force field, she knew she could take it down with barely a blink of an eye.

Safan was sitting on a narrow ledge that apparently served as both bed and chair. His head was down, and he looked asleep. Maurra stepped closer to the cell. Her movements alerted him, and he glanced up.

"Maurra!" He was immediately on his feet, a look of astonishment and relief on his craggy features. "You are well?"

She gave a half shrug when what she really wanted to do was throw her arms around him and tumble to the floor. But there could be vid cameras in here, too, and she didn't want to take the chance. They were in bad enough trouble as it was.

"I am as well as can be expected," she answered softly. "Thank you for saving me. I owe you big time."

The huge Ellinod shook his head. "Don't thank me. It was you who made our escape possible." His eyes raked over her, examining her for any signs of injury or illness. He stopped when he reached her forehead. "Any pain?"

Maurra shook her head. "I'm fine. Once they got the translation device out of my back, my psionic powers were able to reassert themselves. Another day or two of rest, and I'll be almost as good as new." She grinned as she crossed her arms over her chest. The desire to negate the force field was becoming an itch she could barely restrain from scratching. A quick study of the interior of the cell, the pulse polls, and the corridor did not reflect any type of monitoring device that she was familiar with, but it would be safer to assume there would be some sort of equipment to help the Ellinod keep an eye on their prisoners. Lowering her voice, Maurra whispered, "Are we being observed?"

"Yes."

She sighed loudly. Because there was nothing to sit on other than the floor, that's where Maurra sat. She drew her knees up under her chin and clasped her arms around her legs. "Tell me what happened, Safan. What happened after I blasted the Kronners?"

He sat on the floor directly in front of her and crossed his legs. Barely two feet of space separated them, but the hissing, sparkling force field lay directly between them, making itself known every few seconds before settling into temporary transparency.

"You realize that everything we say can and will be used by the Law Keepers against us," he told her.

"What does it matter? We have nothing to hide. Not anymore. They already know everything, or think they do. I doubt there is much we can say to change their minds at this point." She rubbed her eyes and realized that despite her best intentions, she was pushing herself. She needed rest, and she needed to get back to the hospital soon before she collapsed.

Yes, she could use her powers again to re-energize herself, but without sufficient rest, and in her weakened state, the temporary bursts of energy would lessen in strength and duration.

Safan saw her failing. "Lie down, Maurra."

She looked up and gave him a quizzical look.

"Lie down," he repeated. "The floor is warm. You can rest while I fill you in."

She didn't question him. In fact, by stretching out on her side and using one arm as a pillow, Maurra found it to be quite comfortable. "I vaguely remember you or someone saying the Kronners are dead? I know I didn't hit them that hard, or did I?"

"I know you blasted them so hard, the walls of the hold lit up. My ears were ringing, and I was half-blind when I grabbed you and ran from the cell. Bodies were everywhere. Some of them could have been dead. Maybe all of them were still alive, but I wasn't going to stop and check. Not when it could be our only chance to get out of there."

Maurra nodded.

"From previous run-ins with the Kronners, I already had an idea where their shuttle craft were located. By the time I got to the loading dock, one ship had already taken off."

"Vol Brod?"

"It had to be. I threw you into the closest pod and got us away from the ship as quickly as possible." He shook his head. "Something told me to push it, to get as much distance between us and the ship as soon as possible. It was a good thing I did. We were barely out of the blast zone when the Kronners' ship exploded." He gave her an undecipherable look. "Whether or not your psi powers killed any of them is a moot point. I'm certain he rigged the ship to blow."

"Of course. Vol Brod wanted to make sure to cover his tracks," Maurra finished. "Do you think he knows we got away, too?"

Safan shrugged. "I have no idea. I don't even know which direction he took once he left the ship. Once we were free, my main concern was you. You looked dead, Maurra. You were barely breathing. The closest planet I knew that had an adequate medical facility was Kronnaria, but I wasn't about to take you there. There was also a small clinic on Pal Tor Vista's second moon, but it's only set up to take care of the miners. Physical injuries. The doctor there told me he was neither trained nor had the equipment to handle mental injuries like yours."

Maurra gave a slight nod. Little by little, bits and pieces were coming back to her. Fragments of memories during those moments when she drifted in and out of unconsciousness.

"Is that when you brought me here?" she asked.

"Yes."

His complexion grew darker and his expression angrier. He saved her life by bringing her to his home world. But by doing so, he had condemned himself. Maurra sat up and crossed her legs, bending over closer to the force field. "What happened next, Safan?"

It took him a few moments before he could answer. Maurra watched as his jaws clenched and unclenched. His large hands curled into fists in his lap.

"They had seen the live feeds Vol Brod had beamed from the Kronners' ship," he told her. "The moment I managed to land the life pod outside the city, a squad of Law Keepers were waiting. Fortunately, there was no difficulty having you sent directly to the hospital. But I was taken straight to confinement, and from here they read me my sentence."

From the finality in his voice, Maurra felt her own fear growing in her stomach. "What sentence?"

"For breaking any of the Universal Laws," Safan said, "the penalty is the mines."

"Working in the mines? For how long?" she whispered.

The Ellinod closed his eyes, and she would swear she saw him shudder. "For the rest of my life," was the answer.

Chapter Twenty
Visitation

For the rest of my life. Maurra wondered if she'd heard him correctly.

"Safan, are you talking about a life sentence?"

"Yes."

She stared at him. For some odd reason, he seemed resigned to his fate. *To hell with that!* She reached toward him, remembering at the last split-second that a high energy barrier divided them. Her fingertips sizzled on contact. Fortunately she withdrew her hand before her psi powers automatically kicked in to protect her. The barrier would not hurt her, but she would have disrupted the energy field. Things were bad enough as it was without the Ellinod police thinking she was trying to free Safan from his cell.

Biting her lips, she drew in her anger and rising fear. "Safan, that's wrong. I mean, I can see you being sentenced to a labor camp for breaking the law willfully, but we were *forced*, damn it! Your life was at stake. My life and my sanity hung in the balance. We were not allowed any options. If we didn't fuck, one or both of us would be dead by now!"

The Ellinod got to his feet and walked over to the side of holding area, close to one of the pulse poles. "The Universal Laws do not allow exceptions or conditions. Maurra, I knew I would be breaking the law forbidding interspecies fornication.

I even protested, if you remember." He was right. She remembered how he had stood up to the Kronners and The Voice, Vol Brod.

"What are you telling me, Safan? That it was a 'damned if you did, or damned if you didn't' type of situation? Fuck me, and you die in the mines? Don't fuck me, and you die by neuron ray? That is so wrong on so many levels, and you know it. You didn't use intent, and your Tribunal can't prove otherwise." Pounding her fist on the stone floor next to her, Maurra asked, "Is there any way you can appeal?"

The expression on his face said everything. "They have my protest on video, Maurra, just as they have proof of us fornicating afterwards."

They have us on video. Perversely, she wondered if the Ellinod had seen the distant 2-D or close-up 3-D version.

They have proof of us fornicating afterwards. Fornicating. Fucking. *Making love.* Funny how two different people could see the same thing from totally opposite viewpoints. What had Safan said not too long ago? *How much longer do you think we must endure this torment?*

Is that how he thought of what they'd done? As torment?

Something twisted inside her. Something sharp and so painful, tears sprung up in her eyes without warning. Maurra sniffed and bowed her head. "What happens next?" she asked.

"To me? Or to you?"

"Both. Do they put you on trial, or...what?"

"There is no trial. Especially not when there is irrefutable proof. At the moment I'm waiting to be transported to the shuttle that will take me to the *Ver Com.*"

"What's that?"

"The transport ship that will take me to the Bansheer mines."

She looked up. "On Bansheer Prime? Your largest moon?"

Safan nodded. "Has the Neris Orgoran given you your departure information?"

"No. He came to my hospital room and tried to impress me with how important he is."

Her remark got a tiny smile from the Ellinod. "Well? Did it work?"

"Not hardly," she grinned back.

The Ellinod snorted. Immediately the sour look of defeat descended back over his features. "From what I could overhear, things will not go well for you when you return to your headquarters."

"Oh?" Why wasn't she surprised by this bit of news?

"Vol Brod had a signal fed to Jora Manitavi."

"Of course he would," Maurra replied bitterly. "He did it to humiliate your people and mine."

"I think he may have also done it as insurance." Safan grimaced. "In case either of us managed to escape."

It made sense, Maurra had to admit. Vol Brod would not overlook any detail, no matter how small.

"I take it there's a shuttle coming for me, too?"

"Yes. It should arrive sometime late today or early tomorrow morning."

Pressing her fist to her lips, Maurra tried to get her thoughts in order, but her emotions were in turmoil. She didn't want to leave, but she couldn't stay. She had no reason to stay. Even if she found an excuse, Safan would not be here.

Safan. She had to get him out of her system. That was her problem. She had to take the memories of what had happened on board the Kronner ship and put it behind her. Put it past her because she damn sure would never be able to forget it.

"Guess that means by the time I leave, you'll already be gone?"

The beast looked down at the floor. "The shuttle is due to arrive before nightfall."

The knife inside her chest twisted again, slicing through muscle and blood vessels with ease. *Oh, sweetest heavens, what was wrong with her? Why in the hell did the thought of the Ellinod spending the rest of his life in servitude in the mines tear her apart like this?*

Maurra sucked air through her gritted teeth and tried to will away the hot tears burning her eyes. "Safan, what about a plea? Are you allowed to plead your case to the Tribunal?"

"Not this time. Not when they have the vids as proof."

"Exactly!" She stared directly at him. "The vids are proof you broke the laws *under duress!* Doesn't that mean *some*thing?"

"Yes, it does. It means I broke the law," he said with finality.

"Oh, *fuck* your laws and your Tribunal!" Maurra screamed, bending over to beat her fists on the floor in front of her. She got to her feet and straightened up to face the force field head-on. Already her psi powers were coalescing, gradually building and providing her strength with their life-giving tonic.

Safan rushed to place himself directly opposite of her. "No, Maurra. Do not destroy the force field. Don't even try."

"They're going to kill you," she argued, unmindful of the tears sliding down her cheeks. "You screwed me, and they're going to kill you for it!"

"Yes, they are," he murmured in a soothing voice. "But if you try to release me, things will go worse for you, and you know it. We're already an anathema here on my world, as you are now on yours. When you return, you know you'll have to face similar condemnation. Don't..." He reached out until his hand was even with hers and almost brushed the force field. "Don't make things worse for you."

He was still protecting her, she realized. Things were already shit-bad for both of them. The last thing either of them needed to do was to continue to buck the system and make it worse...if it could get any worse.

She stood in front of the invisible shield and forced herself to calm down. To draw her powers back within herself where she could more easily keep them at bay. Intent on concentrating, she almost didn't hear his question.

"What will they do to you?"

It was clear what he meant. What would happen to her once she returned to her own headquarters? Maurra shrugged. "I have no idea."

"Will they imprison you?"

"I don't know, but I'm sure I'll be punished in some manner."

"I fear things will be worse for you." His concern etched every word.

Maurra realized the Ellinod was struggling with something, but for some reason she couldn't sense it. It was possible the force field was blocking her from reading him clearly. Regardless, he was probably right. In the strict context of the law, she was equally guilty for breaking the interspecies fornication law. In addition, she could also be held responsible for the deaths of the Kronners. Even indirectly.

"What does the Jora do with a JoJo who's gone rogue?"

Gone rogue. Funny how the term had a whole new meaning when she was the person it referred to.

"It depends on the infraction," Maurra said. She started to explain that JoJos were rarely stripped of their titles. Once a person was identified with psionic powers, he could either take the job or decline it. But once he accepted the position, it became a lifetime commitment. JoJos didn't retire. They usually didn't live long enough to enjoy that benefit. She started to tell him when the guard appeared at the door.

"The *Ver Com* is here. You must leave," the Ellinod announced, looking at her.

Maurra turned back around to find Safan staring at her. From the intensity of his gaze, she could tell he was drinking her in. Memorizing her. Remembering her. Implanting her so deeply in his mind that she would forever haunt his subconscious. Why he would do so was a mystery.

"I *will* see you again," she promised. "We'll survive this."

Safan gave a nod, giving her the impression he didn't believe her. "Be well, Maurra," he rumbled in that velvety voice. "Please live a long, full life." He started to say more but stopped.

The guard reached for her to urge her to leave. She jerked her arm out of his grasp and tried to follow him out, but it was difficult to see the Ellinod with tears blurring her vision.

Chapter Twenty-One
Jora

Two days later she was on a shuttle heading for the hub on Formehndii. From there she caught the next big tourist cruiser for the Rictus system, and then another smaller transport vessel to complete her journey to the fourth moon circling the planet known as Manitavi.

Maurra watched their approach to the amber brown planet with its nine moons. Eons ago Manitavi had ceased to be a habitable planet, but by then its moons had become a series of substations and landing docks for that region of space. JoJo headquarters was on Jora. Each moon was named after the Manitavese equivalent of its number. Hence, Jora meant "four".

The ship circled the planet and was already on its approach to Jora when a flight attendant came up the aisle and handed Maurra a sealed tablet. The man's face was expressionless, but it was the exact same look she had seen on nearly every face of every person she'd come into contact with since she'd left Ellinod. A bland visage that reflected no emotion whatsoever. It was the face of a person who had either seen one of the Kronner vids, or knew of them.

Maurra broke the seal to read the message.

Jurasu Roja Maurra,

> *Immediately upon arrival, you are ordered to appear before the Jora Cartuum to answer to the following charges set against you. To whit:*
> > ** Deliberate disregard for life (Code 24A)*
> > ** Deliberate fornication with a non-related species (Law 616)*
> > ** Noncompliance with issued orders*
> *You will be allowed to plead your case before sentencing. Remember that failure to follow our directives will be considered an act of treason, and will result in immediate imprisonment, as well as permanent banishment from the Joramansu program.*

It was signed by the Cartuum Prime. Maurra checked the time stamp. It had been issued less than four spacial hours ago. Which meant they were intensely following her progress from Ellinod.

She felt whole and well, although there were times she realized she needed more rest than usual. The sense of being complete and in control had yet to come back to her. The happy little pet, her own special personalization for the incredible ability she was born with, remained lying in the corner somewhere inside her. Lying and watching. Waiting to be called out. Waiting to be let out to play.

Before the ship landed, she spotted Dreeson standing by the gate. She took her time exiting the craft, letting the other passengers off first. Since she had no baggage, she was able to slip through the disembarking tube, bypass the reclamation area, and head straight for the exit.

The magistrate for the Jora Cartuum gave her brown pants and top a disapproving frown. "You know why I'm here," he stated rather than asked.

"Yeah." She shoved the tablet into his chest and the emblem emblazoned there, and kept walking. The man never broke stride, but kept pace beside her. After seeing the JoJo give her another negative glance, Maurra grunted. "Forgive me for not being in uniform. Are you going to add that to my list of charges?"

He didn't reply.

They walked to the tram that would take them directly to the judicial section of headquarters. She noticed how the man kept close to her. He wasn't taking any precautions in the event she tried to escape. The idea was almost funny considering all the chances she'd had up until now to get away.

"Pull in your claws, Maurra. I'm on your side, remember?" he finally remarked.

"Yeah. Must really gall you to have to represent me."

"Shove it, Maurra. A strong word of caution. Don't try to deliberately piss off the Cartuum."

"Or what?" She stopped abruptly and whirled around to face him. "What can they do to me that they haven't already decided to do?" she challenged him hotly. "Two of those charges are bogus, yet I can't refute them—"

"The vids clearly back every charge," Dreeson argued.

"Grot shit! I did not kill those Kronners. I negated them, yes, but it was Tramer Vol Brod who blew up the ship and killed them! And as for that idiotic noncompliance issue..." She realized her anger had been seething inside her ever since she had awakened on Ellinod and discovered Safan's fate. Since then it had steadily grown in heat and combustibility until it was at the point where she felt like she could barely contain her rage. Dreeson must have noticed she was close to the melting point and visibly reined back.

"Tramer Vol Brod?" he repeated.

"Didn't the magistrates wonder during the entire time I was being held captive that *someone* was responsible for kidnapping me?"

"We assumed it was the Kronners," Dreeson admitted. "Right after we received the first feed, we dispatched a liaison to Kronnaria to affect your release."

Maurra rolled her eyes. "I bet you accomplished a lot with that tactic," she almost sneered.

Dreeson shrugged. They had resumed their walk to the tram and were now waiting for its arrival. "They repeatedly denied involvement until we showed them the vid."

"After which they repeatedly denied having hatched the scheme in the first place." Sighing loudly, she tucked an errant bit of hair over her ear. To her shock, a tear dropped onto the back of her hand.

The tram arrived, and they took the front compartment. Once the door closed behind them, Maurra collapsed on one of the seats. Dreeson chose to remain standing and hold onto a balance pole. A couple of minutes passed in silence. Maurra watched the view from the window change as they left the space center and headed into the city.

"You're exhausted. It's a miracle you survived."

She glanced up at the man. "Well, it's nice to see your powers of observation are still as astute as ever."

"That's why you haven't tried to escape before now."

"Wow. And perceptive, too."

Dreeson gave a little growl of irritation. "Gods damn it! I'm not the enemy, Maurra! I saw what Vol Brod made you do! I know how difficult it must have been—"

She turned on him with renewed fire. "You know *nothing* about what it was like, so don't try to placate me! You weren't there. You didn't have to endure..." She swallowed, afraid to go on. "The only reason you're here is because you and the others are just itching to condemn what I did because you want the integrity of the Jora Cartuum to remain spotless. You want to prove to the galactic councils that even a JoJo isn't above punishment for breaking the law. Well, that's all fine and good, Dreeson. I'll take my bitter pills for breaking the one law, *the one law!* But not for the other shit, do you hear me? And I want you to promise me that Tramer Vol Brod will be held accountable for everything he did."

She stared up at him and waited, daring him, needing to see how far he was willing to commit himself, and how much he'd sold his soul to the Cartuum.

"We used to be friends once," Maurra continued in a calmer voice. *We used to be lovers, back before I outpaced you promotion-wise, and you turned to enlist in the magistrate program in a fit of jealousy. Watching me being fucked by the Ellinod must have sickened you more than anyone else who watched.* "I'm not asking for absolution, Dree. I just want the other two charges dismissed."

She had no idea her voice had trailed off until Dreeson questioned her with his eyebrows. "And what? What else did you want to say?" he said.

"Only that I have no lingering guilt over what I did. For what I was forced to do," she admitted.

It was as if an immense weight was suddenly lifted from her shoulders. Yes, she was guilty of fornication. But, no, she wasn't the least bit sorry for doing it. She wanted Dreeson to be the first to know the truth. The council of magistrates would find out next. And eventually, hopefully, sometime in the future, Safan would learn of her confession.

I'm not ashamed of what I did with you, Safan. Of what we did. Neither will I forget it.

The sun broke over the horizon. Its orange rays struck the tram's windows, turning them into sheets of gold as the vehicle slowed to enter the access area of the magistrate court. Within the hour she would discover what her fate would be and what her future would hold. Yet, for some reason, Maurra felt no fear or no trepidation.

In fact, she felt wonderfully...free.

Chapter Twenty-Two
Sentencing

Maurra was allowed to go back to her apartment and clean up before she presented herself to the Cartuum for sentencing. Standing in front of the mirror, she stared long and hard at the image reflected in it. Although she didn't consider herself vain, she knew she looked damn good in the JoJo uniform. The emblazoned crest on the front of her jerkin resembled the ball of psion energy when it formed on her forehead. In the morning sunlight, it almost looked alive. The only thing missing was her pistol, which had been converted into so much space dust when the Kronner ship exploded. Technically, the pistol didn't contain any power. All of her power came from her and was streamed into the gun. The weapon was attuned to her brain waves, and she was able to adjust the flow and strength of her psi energy through it with a greater amount of accuracy than when she simply let her powers loose.

Grimacing, she left the apartment and rejoined Dreeson, who was waiting for her outside. The time for petty sniping at each other was long over. She didn't know whether the man had volunteered to be her guard cum escort, or if he'd been assigned to it. Either way it didn't matter. To be truthful, she was glad he would be standing beside her when the final ruling came down.

"I'm going to miss seeing you in the reds," the man said as they walked the short distance back to the judicial building. She didn't answer, preferring to remain silent as she mentally and emotionally dealt with the upcoming event.

Every step felt like she was walking a pathway to nowhere. If the triumvirate ruled on all three charges set up against her, she could face permanent imprisonment. If they threw away the two charges she was innocent of and settled on the third one...

"Straight up, Dree. What's the worst that could happen to me?"

"Other than sending you to a prison moon for the remainder of your life? That kind of worst?"

"What's the penalty for screwing an Ellinod?" she asked straight out.

"Well...if you do manage to get them to drop the other two charges, I'd say you can pretty much plan on being stripped of your title and kicked out of the corp."

Maurra swallowed hard. She had expected as much. The magistrates were not known for leniency to one of their own. In fact, they often televised an errant JoJo's punishment just to let the rest of the inhabited galaxies know that even JoJos weren't above the laws. She'd never watched or witnessed any of the sentencings, but she knew they could be brutal.

She snorted. For years she had kept a low profile, doing her job and helping maintain the law. But now, in the space of a few short weeks, her face and her body were known throughout the galaxy. *Guess my days of anonymity are at an end.*

Around them, the walkways were bustling. They were in the heart of Jora, in the main hub of activity for all JoJos. Some passed them, on their way to a new assignment. Others had just landed and were seeking rest before accepting a new assignment. None of them, Maurra noticed, greeted her as they passed. Most, if not all, kept their faces averted to avoid possible eye contact.

They all know. They've all seen the vids, or were aware of them, and they've already pronounced their judgment on me regardless of the circumstances. For my punishment, in their eyes I'm no longer deemed worthy to wear this uniform or to call myself a JoJo.

She and Dreeson entered the small lift, which took them up and over to the main judicial chambers. As they exited the tube, they were greeted by a small squadron of JoJos, one of whom opened one of the large crystalline doors.

Inside, the main chamber was packed. As she entered the large room, every eye shifted to her, and the place went totally silent. Maurra stood in stunned disbelief for several seconds as she stared at the number of people waiting to see what she would receive in retribution. Dreeson gave her arm a little nudge.

"Move on, Maurra. Let's get this over with."

Pressing her lips together, she continued toward the dais where the magistrates sat, their gazes also locked onto her. When she reached the small podium that faced them, Dreeson gave her arm a squeeze and left her to take his place at the end of the row. The magistrates wasted no time getting started.

"Jurasu Roja Maurra, you have been brought here today to face a jury of your peers and to answer to the charges brought against you. Are you fully aware of those charges?"

She nodded. "Yes, Council. I am also aware that two of the charges are bogus, and I request that they be stricken from this hearing. I also request that any punishment being considered because of the severity of those charges be removed from consideration."

The three men glanced over at Dreeson, who nodded. The first magistrate, a man Maurra had never met, considered something on the table in front of him. She assumed it was a tablet.

"We are not above correcting those charges if you can prove them to be incorrect," the man said. "We have been informed by your defense council that you were personally not responsible for the deaths of the Kronners, is that correct?"

We have been informed by your defense council that you were personally not responsible for the deaths of the Kronners. Dreeson must have been debriefed while she was getting ready.

"That is correct, Your Graces. I did pulse the Kronners, but not enough to kill them. Tramer Vol Brod, who is responsible for kidnapping me and instigating this whole ordeal, managed to escape in a life pod moments before the Ellinod and I were able to make our escape as well. We were not far from the Kronner ship when it exploded."

"Tramer Vol Brod." The left magistrate made a notation on his tablet. "We will make note of the man as a person of interest."

Which meant, in JoJo talk, there would be an all-points bulletin put out on him. Once he was found, he would be pulled in and questioned. And ultimately released. JoJo justice. They couldn't convict a person solely on another person's word, even if that other person was a JoJo. There had to be evidence. Hard, solid, and irrefutable evidence. And all that evidence was now molecules in space.

The head magistrate frowned. "Why did you leave the ship? Why didn't you take the Kronners prisoners?"

"I was unconscious, Your Graces. The Kronners had placed a translation device on my spine which caused severe pain and unconsciousness whenever I tried to implement my psi powers. That's why I was initially unable to free myself and the Ellinod. I was forced to wait for the right opportunity to throw my powers at them in order to give us a chance to escape."

The magistrate on the right leaned forward. "So what you're saying is you risked your life to save the Ellinod by using your powers against the Kronners?"

"Yes."

Three identical orbs of light red light instantly appeared on all three magistrates' faces. Maurra looked to see a fourth orb coalescing on Dreeson's forehead, too. At that same moment she could feel them sensing her, trying to read her. It was well known that psions were unable to read minds directly, but they could read emotions. Their psi energy could tell them if a person was fabricating a lie or being truthful. It wasn't until the magistrate on the left spoke that she felt her first jolt of fear.

"You say you were rendered unconscious after you overpowered the Kronners, is that correct, Jurasu Roja Maurra?"

"Yes. The Ellinod carried me to the escape pod with him."

"And the device on your back, it had a direct effect on how you used your powers, correct?"

"That's true."

"Then you don't know for certain that you didn't kill the Kronners, do you?"

Her stomach lurched. From the looks on their faces, they sensed her reaction.

"No. I don't know for certain that I didn't kill the Kronners."

"Your Graces." Dreeson stepped forward and waited for permission to speak. The magistrates nodded for him to continue. "I wish to remind you that supposition is not allowed at a sentencing. To assume some of the Kronners may have been killed when Maurra used her powers is wrong and therefore should be stricken from the record. The Kronners are dead because another person killed them. Period. The ship was less than a day's journey from its home world. By continuing that supposition, had the ship been left alone, the Kronners could have eventually been discovered and revived, or in some other way rescued. You cannot place the burden of their deaths on Maurra's head when you yourself do not have actual proof."

The threesome went into a huddle for immediate discussion. When they eventually broke, Maurra could feel a small sense of relief even before the head magistrate spoke.

"Point conceded, Joramansu Dreeson. The charge of murder is stricken."

An enormous rush of relief surged through her. She could hope again. With the charge of murder removed, so was the chance of receiving the penalty of permanent incarceration and a possible death sentence.

"May I continue?" Dreeson continued. He received another nod. "The charge of noncompliance to orders is ridiculous. How can Maurra be accused of not returning to base when she was ordered to, when she was being held as a captive?"

"I can answer that," the magistrate on the left answered. "She was ordered back to Jora after completing her previous assignment. Instead, she chose to stay on Cura-Cura. Had she followed orders and caught the next flight out, she would not have been taken captive by the Kronners."

Dreeson shot a look at Maurra, who slowly nodded. Yeah, they got her there. But at the time she was exhausted and felt like she deserved a few hours of R and R to unwind. That's why she'd skipped the last freighter heading out that would be able to drop her off at the Manitavi hub, and instead sought out a cold drink at the nearest bar.

The bar where she first saw Safan. The bar she had left, only to see him being attacked by the Kronners.

Fate.

Maurra conceded. "You are right, Your Graces. I did disregard orders and choose to remain on Cura-Cura for a while longer, which allowed the Kronners to follow through with their plans."

The main magistrate grunted. "So the charge of disobedience stays. That leaves the charge of fornicating with an alien species." He and the other two men gave her a strong look. "How do you plead?"

"Guilty," she answered without hesitation.

"Very well. Jurasu Roja Maurra, are you ready for sentencing?"

"Yes, Your Graces."

The magistrate on the right cleared his throat. "Jurasu Roja Maurra, it is this council's decision that your rights, title, and distinction as a JoJo be permanently dissolved. Have you any words regarding this decision?"

There it was—short, succinct, and bitter. She was no longer a JoJo.

"No, Your Graces. I clearly understand."

"Very well." The middle magistrate gestured Dreeson over. "Joramansu Dreeson, please see to it that Maurra is removed from Jora base within the next twelve hours."

"Yes, Your Graces."

Maurra started to turn to head out of the chamber when the magistrate interjected one more time.

"We cannot control what you do with your psi powers, Maurra, but remember this. They are a powerful weapon. Therefore, whenever you use them, they will be considered as such. You may not be able to enforce the laws, but you are still responsible for upholding them. So use your powers wisely."

She nodded, unable to reply because of the heat flushing her face. Fighting back the tears, Maurra strode stiffly out of the hall with Dreeson in tow.

She was no longer a JoJo, and she had twelve hours to clear all of her things out of her apartment. Which meant she had to find a new place to live. A new world to live on. And a job.

When all her life she had trained to be nothing but a JoJo, she now had to cultivate a new skill in a place where she could live in relative obscurity.

From here on out, life was going to be hell.

Chapter Twenty-Three
Riot

She needed a new last name. Momentarily surprised and stuck for an answer, Maurra had replied with the first name to pop into her head.

"Safan. Maurra Safan." Because of her circumstances, she figured it wouldn't have been safe to use her real name.

The apartment manager nodded and jotted the information down in her book as she handed the room key over to Maurra. For sixty-six creds and a first and last name, anyone could rent a ramshackle abode for a month. It was as simple as that.

She was on Alintarus, a tiny planet in the Duro Chivvan system, and a short two-hour flight via shuttle pod from Jora. Although it was relatively close to Jora, Alintarus was, in many ways, a backwards planet. Mainly agricultural, it had been settled by several humanoid species strictly for the purpose of growing produce on its nearly limitless land to sell to other worlds where others of their kind existed.

The largest city, or rather town, was Belunerr. An hour by rented slider found Maurra in Vi Worr, a tiny burg on the outskirts of one of the major crops. Maurra easily found work as a reaper, helping in the fields. It was manual labor, hard and tedious, but it had three things going for it. She was in no danger of using of her power, and thus drawing attention to herself. There was no background check done on her, as the turnover rate for this kind of back-breaking job ran at almost ninety percent. And technology was at least two decades behind the norm, if not more. The vid monitors on this world were incapable of receiving transmissions from more advanced galaxies, which meant the chances were good no one here had seen the Kronner's vids.

All she needed to do was keep a low profile, and life might be tolerable. Key word being "might."

Maurra dumped the last carton of supplies she'd brought with her on the floor and straightened up. She grimaced as she looked around the apartment that would be her home for the next...what? Days? Months? Years? It was barely two rooms. The bedroom was also the living area and kitchen. The bathroom was the only other door, besides the front door.

She brushed the hair from her face. She felt gritty, dirty, hot, and sweaty. Alintarus was a sub-tropical planet, lush and green, with rich soil similar in texture to coarse sand. Her blouse lay plastered to her skin. A window fan pumped barely cool air into the room. Otherwise there was nothing to break the heat from the mid-morning sun.

Walking over to the window, she tried to wipe some of the grime from the single pane. The view from the second story was of the edge of town. Not a hundred yards beyond that, fertile fields awaited. Harvest would be here soon. She had arrived just in time.

An elderly Gori Vicorrian exited a shop and limped out of view. The Vicorri system was a good dozen or so light years from this place, which made her wonder how many inhabitants on Alintarus were fugitives like herself. Fugitives. Cast-offs. Pariahs.

Maurra lifted her blouse to let the fan blow up her chest and over her bared breasts. It provided a moment of respite. She was to start work tomorrow morning. If she thought this was muggy weather now, she knew she'd be miserable by this time tomorrow after just a few hours of labor.

She glanced out the window again. The sun was shining. The wind was blowing. It was a picturesque landscape. Had she been a casual visitor, she might have looked upon the scene and thought everything was right and good, and life was filled with unlimited hope. Maurra snorted at the irony. Funny how she'd spent most of her life preparing herself, training endlessly, and learning to expect the unexpected when performing her duties. And in the end, it was being the target of a man she had sent to the K'ro Kriall penal colony that had brought about her downfall.

She was no longer a JoJo, but she would always have her psi powers.

And her memories.

Tears clogged her throat. They always did now, every time she thought of him.

I see the sun. You see the dark. I feel the wind on my face. You will never smell fresh air again.

She sniffed and wiped her cheeks with her fingers. When she had awakened in the Ellinod hospital, she had believed she'd been the one who had made the greatest sacrifice in order to get her and Safan free from the Kronners. She knew she was wrong now. She hadn't made the greatest sacrifice. Even if she had died, nothing would be able to match what Safan was enduring. With death, her suffering would be over. Safan was suffering in ways she couldn't imagine, and he would never find an end to it. Not for as long as he lived.

Do you blame me, Safan? Do you ever stop to think that if I hadn't been there, that your fate would have been different?

Do you ever think of me?

Sexually speaking, Maurra truly believed she was ruined, but not in an unhealthy way. Although her total number of sexual encounters were not as many as people would assume, they had been mostly unsatisfying. Usually one-night stands meant to fulfill a craving or a need. A sexual act that rarely succeeded in doing that. And for the one or two people who had almost miraculously wrung an orgasm out of her, one of whom had been Dreeson, the encounters overall had left her empty and distant.

Long ago she had realized she wanted more than a hard fuck. She also wanted intimacy. She wanted tenderness and caring. Most of all, she wanted permanence. She wanted to believe her being with her partner was of paramount importance to the both of them. That parting would leave cold, immense, emotional holes in the psyche. Dreeson never gave her that feeling. Neither had any of the others she had chosen.

But the one male she hadn't selected...he had come close. So awfully close, it was painful to think about it. The one male who hadn't been her choice, but the choice of a group of sleazy Kronners. Even before they had fucked, he had touched her with a gentleness that at first shocked and surprised her. After that first time, even with the translation device chewing through her spinal cord, Maurra sensed an honest affection. This man would never mistreat her. He would never lie to her. He would never give her any reason to think she wasn't important to him.

The other night she had tried to pleasure herself, but she'd failed miserably. It took focusing on her memories of Safan and their lovemaking before she had gotten any sort of meager release. In the hours afterward, she had come to the conclusion that her body would never respond again to a man of her kind. If her future looked pathetic, her sex life was definitely the pits.

Her stomach cramped. She had no idea what time it was, but she needed to eat, especially with a full day of manual labor facing her tomorrow. Maurra patted her pockets to find her key. Locking her apartment door behind her, she headed for the stairs. There hadn't been much for her to clean out once she'd been ejected from her apartment on Jora. If someone tried to break into her place here, they might be surprised at what they'd find among her possessions, but there wasn't much worth taking that they could sell.

At the thought, Maurra wondered what kind of crime Alintarus saw on a regular basis. She bet the bars were the main trouble-making hot spots.

Forget it, Maurra. It doesn't pertain to you anymore.

She silently growled. Seeing worlds through JoJo eyes would be a very difficult habit to break.

The landlady was in her office. The humanoid Xvasus saw Maurra walk by and gave a little wave. Maurra managed to paste a smile on her face and waved back. There was no sense asking the woman where she could find a place to eat. Vi Worr was so tiny, Maurra could easily walk the town's perimeter in a short amount of time.

She exited into the heat-soaked day and automatically took a deep breath. She could smell dirt and metal, and green growing plants. And smoke. Not ordinary smoke. Smoke scented with something cooking on an open fire.

Her nose led her down the one street in town until she reached an open patio between two stores. Underneath a large awning were several tables, some already bearing patrons. Their mutterings came over the Ellinodian translation device she still wore on her wrist as garbled speech. They glanced over at her standing at the entrance, then dismissed her to go back to their discussion and meals. Maurra felt her nervousness ease a bit. They didn't recognize her. It would take her some time to accept that, too. But when it finally occurred, and she had no doubt that sooner or later she would be outed, she would have no choice but to move on to the next backwater planet or moon or asteroid.

Yes, she had thought about toughing it out. Seeing how long before prejudices subsided, and the planet could finally accept her as one of the other lost souls working the bigra grain fields. But then reality gave her a swift kick in the butt to remind her that prejudices, especially those upheld by "law," never subsided. And they never went away.

"You want to eat?"

Maurra jumped, startled by the voice at her elbow. She looked down to see a vavelt staring up at her. The creature wore an apron and a questioning stare.

"If you want to eat, take a seat." The vavelt flashed its incisors and scurried away. Maurra found a table as far away from the other patrons as possible and sat down. The table was greasy to the touch, but the odors wafting through the air smelled fabulous. The kitchen was a tiny hut made of scrap metal which sat on the edge of the patio. A stovepipe jutting through the roof was the source of all the wonderful odors.

Again, guilt clutched her gut and squeezed. *How are you doing, Safan? Are you eating enough? Are you uninjured? How are the other prisoners treating you?* For the hundredth time, she wished she could send her powers across the galaxy in order to check on him. Her range was far, but it wasn't strong enough to traverse space.

The kitchen door burst open, and the vavelt she'd met earlier waddled over to her. The creature climbed up on the other chair at Maurra's table and perched two of its hands on its hips.

"What will it be? Corfu buds or mordri?"

Maurra gave her a confused look. "I don't know. I'm new here."

"Are you a veggo or a carniv?"

"A what?"

"Plant eater or meat eater?"

The vision of a nice juicy brolto burger popped into her head. "Uhh, meat eater."

The vavelt nodded and yelled over its shoulder. "Slab of mordri at table two!" Back at Maurra, the creature said, "I'll bring you a mug of proctering juice, unless you'd like something harder."

"No. No thanks. The juice sounds fine."

The little creature jumped off the chair and made its way over to the next table full of customers.

Maurra wiped her hands on her thighs. She wished she'd thought about washing her hands before heading out. Too late now. A glint of light off the tiny translator still embedded in her wrist caught her eye. The hospital staff had offered to remove it once the doctor's orders came down to release her, but she had declined. Without her JoJo uniform with its translator woven throughout the fabric, she'd be lost in a sea of indecipherable noise without the little device. It wouldn't be as strong or as capable as the one she was used to, but it was better than nothing until she could afford a better one. And considering what the pay was here on Vi Worr, that might take some time.

A blaring sound erupted from the depths of the kitchen. Someone turned it down until Maurra could make out a single voice speaking in a sing-song tone. She couldn't see the source of the voice, but she assumed it was an old-fashioned radio device. Someone had turned it on to get the latest news or whatever.

"...JoJos have offered to intervene in the riot, but officials from the mines have declined."

JoJos? What? What mines? Leaning over her table, Maurra raised her wrist closer to her ear and tried to concentrate on the broadcast.

"At last count, eight bodies have been recovered. As a result, Ellinod supervisors are refusing to open the shafts down into the lower depths until the rioters have surrendered."

She was on her feet without being aware of it.

"Change your mind?" a little voice by her knee asked.

Maurra gestured toward the kitchen. "What's that about the mines?"

"You mean on the news? There's been a riot over in the Bansheer system." The vavelt shrugged. "I don't know much more than that. Why are you asking? You got stock in the mines? I got stock in them. I hope to make enough off that billir so I can buy myself a little place and retire someday. Hey! Where are you going? You want me to cancel your order?"

Maurra never heard the question. A little voice inside her said she had to get to Bansheer Prime as soon as possible, and somehow she had to stop the riot. Safan's life may depend on it. How she knew he was still alive, she couldn't explain. Neither could she explain how she knew he needed her now more than ever before. She just knew it, the same way she knew, for some unexplainable reason, that her life depended on reaching him, as well.

Chapter Twenty-Four
Mission

Maurra barely had enough creds to buy the old trade ship, but it was the best she could do on such short notice. An unexpected plus—it was exactly what she needed. At first glance, the ship, named *Lorrmandi II*, appeared to be just a few clicks shy of retirement. The engines needed a complete overhaul, but they blew without any noticeable danger signs when she'd tested them. In addition, both the interior and exterior looked as though someone had blowtorched them. Still, the craft was built for interstellar travel, which meant it was sturdy and very well preserved, despite its age and appearance.

The captain's chair was the old standard model—a raised cushion in the middle of the deck overlooking the main front view screen. There were no cuffs, no extensions, nothing to help her facilitate running the vessel from any other part of the ship other than the bridge.

Throwing herself into the worn, padded seat, Maurra strapped herself in and pulled up the driving console from beside one of the wide arms. It deftly locked it into place, and she began warming up the dual engines. Next she punched in her destination, which was relayed to the small landing tower at the far end of Belunerr. This tiny strip stood on the complete opposite end of town from where the larger and more modern landing port was located. From past experience, she knew she'd get a better deal on a used ship if she scoured the smaller bays, and stayed clear of the commercial area.

"*Lorrmandi II*, you are clear for takeoff," a voice buzzed from overhead.

"Confirm. *Lorrmandi II* out," Maurra called back. "All right, Lorri. Let's see what you've got."

"My name is *Lorrmandi II*," the onboard computer calmly corrected her. Maurra noted that the ship replied in standard Terrenglish, which meant the computer had been upgraded to respond in the language it was commanded in. That was good.

"My name is Maurra, and I'm your new captain. And if I want to call you Lorri, you'll answer to Lorri. That's an order."

"Yes, Captain," the computer replied.

The engines fired. Just as they had earlier, they gave a distinctive little second burst.

"Destination locked in. Let's go, Lorri."

"Yes, Captain."

To Maurra's surprise, the little vessel rose as gently as a bubble on the wind. Within seconds she was clear of the planet's gravitational pull.

"Ready to initiate hyper light drive," the ship's computer intoned.

"Then let's do it."

The ship shuddered as its engines opened up to faster-than-light speed. Maurra watched as space exploded into a million colors like blossoming pyrotechnics. It was a sight she never tired of watching. A few minutes and several star systems slid by before she roused herself from the beautiful, almost hypnotic effect.

"Give me an ETA."

"Estimated distance to the Bansheer system, fourteen point three clicks."

"Confirmed. Let's come out of hyper light when we come within one full click of our targeted destination, all right, Lorri?"

"Confirmed, Captain."

Fourteen clicks. Maurra mentally estimated that would be a little over eight hours. Barring any interference or unexpected happenings, she might be able to get in some rest. Heavens knew she needed it.

And something to eat.

"Crap." At the thought of food, her stomach resumed gurgling mode. In her hurry to leave Alintarus, she still hadn't grabbed a decent bite to tide her over.

Unbuckling herself from the seat, Maurra walked to the rear of the vessel where the so-called "living area" was located, separated from the bridge by a folding wall. Originally, the *Lorrmandi II* had been a Tygrecian vessel. A low-end model, to be exact, but since the Trygrecia were a large hominid species nearly ten feet tall, smaller bipeds like herself had plenty of room to maneuver in what would have been cramped accommodations for them.

The food prep area was adjacent to the bathing stall. Tucked into the corner was the toilet facility. Maurra eyed the slanted receptacle bowl standing nearly chest high and sighed. She'd worry about surmounting that obstacle later. Right now her attention was on the locker areas where the supplies would be kept.

She checked the lower shelves first, but she wasn't surprised to find them bare. Neither was there anything in the upper galley, from what she could see. On a hunch, she detoured to the rear of the craft where she found several survival packets inside the minuscule life pod that had been overlooked. A glance at the packaging told her nothing. She couldn't read the language. And even if she could, would she try eating the contents if she knew what they were?

Fuck it. As long as it doesn't kill me.

One silverish envelope contained a yellowish paste. Maurra immediately recognized the ration as bruulu. Many planets used bruulu as a main staple in the diet rations for their military units. The stuff was made to last for years. No telling how old these packets were, but she figured anything was better than starving.

On a guess, she opened another packet marked with different symbols. Grokksin, dried and jerked until it was like eating slabs of brick-shaped dirt. But it, like the bruulu, was packed with protein and vitamins. Healthy stuff. Stuff good enough to stave off starvation. Too bad there was absolutely no taste to it to enjoy.

She scarfed down two packets of each, along with a tube of water. There'd been no time to supply the ship, much less check out any of the vessel's other conveniences. But once she rescued Safan from the mines —

Maurra froze. *All right, woman. You've finally admitted it. Maybe in the back of your mind it's been your intention all along, to somehow get Safan away from those deadly mines, but all you had been lacking was an excuse. Well, now you have one. But have you thought ahead as to what you'll do once you rescue him?*

No, damn it. She had never planned ahead for things. She'd never had to. She had always been a spur-of-the-moment sort of girl. When she'd been a JoJo, her ultimate "destination," per se, had always been to do the job she'd been assigned. How she went about accomplishing her task had never been an issue, as long as it was legal. Whatever idea struck her at the time, she'd followed through with it. That was why she'd been so damn good at her job. Her instincts had never failed her. Go with the gut and get it over with.

All right. She was going with her gut again, but this time she didn't have a badge in the center of her chest to give her open and unrestricted access to the mines. In fact, the Ellinod had refused any help from the JoJos, which could only mean one thing. They had to be covering something up.

Or...

They wanted to wash away the taint of the Kronner vids as quickly as possible, and with the JoJos there, their presence might prevent that from happening.

Screw it. She wasn't a JoJo any longer, so they couldn't hold that over her. It would be interesting to see how this whole drama played out once she landed. The only thing that worried her was Safan's health and state of mind.

If she saved him —

When! When she saved him!

When she saved him, would he agree to leave the mines and come with her?

Maurra shook her head. She couldn't go there. She couldn't imagine what she would do next if he refused her.

A yawn overtook her. With a little less than eight hours to kill, Maurra let her training take over. If she was going to face heavens knew how many Ellinod and their weapons, not to mention rioting prisoners, she'd need as much rest as possible in order to build up her reserves so she would be ready. Already she could feel her muscles start to unknot as her belly rejoiced.

The rear area of the galley floor slid away to reveal the bed below. There was a single musty blanket on top of the inflated mattress. Climbing over the warm pallet, she called out, "Lorri, wake me in thirteen clicks," and stretched out.

She never heard the ship's reply.

Chapter Twenty-Five
Bansheer

Maurra awoke on her own before the computer roused her. Stretching out the kinks, she realized with pleasant surprise that her sense of time had returned to her. It was another sign she was getting stronger. Getting back to normal.

There was a cleansing chamber tucked into the corner between the galley and supply lockers. Because it was made for a larger species, it gave her ample room to enjoy a long dousing, as well as wash her hair. It was amazing how much more human she felt when it was over.

On the other hand, the clothing synthesizer was a bit snarky, giving her half the coverage she normally wore, but it was enough. At least the top and pants were clean and stain-free, and covered the essential parts of her body. Maurra had no problem tossing her old things into the incinerator. Grabbing a tube of water, she ambled back to the captain's chair. Sensing Maurra's departure from the area, the ship slid the flooring back into place over the bed.

"Lorri, ETA to Bansheer."

"One point six clicks."

Silently Maurra mouthed the exact answer as it was given to her by the ship and grinned when they matched. "Thank you, Lorri."

"My duty, Captain."

With a little more than an hour until touchdown, she needed to find out where the mines were located and start figuring out one or two hasty retreat routes, just in case. Maurra called up what maps the ship had stored, one of which was the Ellinod system. That didn't seem unusual to her, considering the wealth of gemstones that came from there.

So far so good. She was almost there, and she knew she had the capability to get Safan out of that hellhole as long as she watched what she was doing. That left her with two other problems—coming up with a legitimate excuse to free the Ellinod, and then figuring out what they were going to do once they left the mines.

One step at a time. One problem at a time. Just like old times.

The little ship shuddered again, indicating they were leaving hyper light and re-entering normal space. The rainbow of rich, jewel-like colors solidified and became hard pinpoints of light. At the far left side of the viewscreen the dark brown sphere that was her target slowly focused into view.

"Lorri, steer course for Bansheer Prime."

"Calculating orbit."

"Unidentified space craft, please respond with I.D.," a strange deep voice suddenly requested over the comm. She was nearing where the mines were located.

"Lorri?"

"Communications are open, Captain."

Maurra took a deep breath. "Planet Bansheer, this is *Lorrmandi II.* I'm experiencing engine problems and need to land to affix repairs immediately."

"Negative, Lorrmandi II," said the live voice. "This is Bansheer Prime, a penal mining colony. You are not to land. Instead, use the coordinates we're sending you now. Bansheer

Four is the next closest inhabited moon where you can repair your craft."

"Negative that," Maurra said, adding what she hoped sounded like panic to the tone of her voice. "I think my hyper light drive has become unstable. What if I land on your back side?"

An unstable hyper light drive was dangerous to both ships' crews and to anything else within implosion distance, a range of normally two to three thousand meters. In almost every instance, it was a universal gesture of goodwill to allow a ship fearing a hyper light backwash immediate access to land so that its crew could safely evacuate. Maurra knew her asking to land on the back side of the moon would not be considered an unreasonable request.

"Permission granted, *Lorrmandi II*. Please set a periphery of a minimum of ten thousand meters. Uploading a suggested target landing area. If all ends well, please send a relay back. Otherwise we will keep a signal beamed in your area in case you need help."

"Thanks," Maurra called back. "Closing communications."

She shut off the main transmission and concentrated on landing at the designated spot assigned to her. It was all fine and good, as far as she was concerned. Even better was the fact that they were keeping an eye on the ship. With their attention divided between the riot at the mines, and the occasional glance at the space craft, there was little chance they would spot a lone figure skulking about in the darkness.

And speaking of skulking...

Maurra glanced down at her simple outfit. Fortunately the clothes she was wearing were a dark color, which would help her blend in. But the only other clothing she owned was back on Alintarus. In fact, everything else she owned was sitting in a box in the tiny apartment she'd rented.

A tiny smile lifted the corners of her mouth. *Wonder if I'll make it back in time for my first day of work?* At the thought, she gave a short laugh. To be brutally honest, at the moment she didn't give a fat carzak's ass if she ever returned there.

She landed the ship on the surface with barely a bump. Throwing off her harness, she got to her feet and took a few seconds to bounce on the balls of her feet, acclimating herself to the gravity.

"Lorri, I'm leaving the ship for an unknown amount of time. Do you have a remote device where I can let you know my location?"

To her right, a tiny drawer slid out from the wall. Inside was a slender cylinder, no more than half the size and width of her little finger. Picking it up, Maurra stared at it for a moment.

"Where's the best place to put this?" she asked the computer.

"It adheres to the skin," the ship replied.

The memory of the translation device buried inside her spine caused her to wince, when she suddenly got an idea. Lifting up her shirt, she placed the cylinder underneath her right breast. Nestled there, it didn't feel uncomfortable, plus she wouldn't have to worry about losing it if she stuck it in her pocket.

And it wouldn't interfere with her powers.

"Lorri, I want you to fire your engines in a random pattern while I'm gone. Make it look like someone is working on them, got that?"

"Yes, Captain. Anything else?"

"Yeah. If they call for me, tell them I'm in the back engine compartment and will answer when I can. Keep putting them off."

"Yes, Captain."

Opening the short ramp, Maurra braced herself. Being a mining moon, Bansheer Prime had been given an atmosphere rather than building the usual enormous, self-sustaining domes to accommodate the inhabitants. Being a penal colony, there were no other cities or towns. Those who were employed there, and those who were not registered as a prisoner, shuttled between the moon and Ellinod on a daily basis.

Bansheer Prime was nothing more than a huge, elliptical rock rich with billir crystals. One could literally pick up the gemstones from the surface. But the more prized crystals came from deep within the mines, down where the pressures created elaborate, flame-like ruptures within the brown mineral.

Before the ramp hit the packed dirt, she was out of the ship and running toward the horizon where the above-ground offices for the penitentiary were located.

Chapter Twenty-Six
Welcoming

The main mine entrance was ringed by an artificially created crater, whose walls rose as high as fifty meters in some areas. Another ring of lights the size of small asteroids hovered nearly a hundred meters above the crater, keeping the whole area in perpetual daylight. There was only one road going in and out, and traffic was regulated by a gate of high-density plasma jets.

The landing pad for those employed by the mining companies and penal institute was less than a half-mile away. It was a safety measure, having it that far from the main entrance, to dispel escaping prisoners from making a run for it. There was nothing but flat, open surface between the mines and the pad, making the convicts easy targets.

By the same token, crystals brought up from the depths of the mine were loaded into vats containing byridic almaf acid that would eat away the residual rock, leaving only the crystals in near-pristine condition. The vats would then be trundled through a second gate where loaders would place them into specialized compartments. The compartments would subsequently be loaded onto ships heading back to Ellinod. If anyone tried to make a break for freedom that way, they were doomed before they ever started. For one thing, no one could survive the acid if they tried to hide in a vat. But if by some miracle the escaping prisoner tried via some special type of body suit, they wouldn't make it past the plasma gates. Plasma radiation literally melted tissue from the bone.

The mines were fortified to the hilt, and to date, no one had ever managed to escape.

Maurra used the cover of darkness to hide her advance toward the crater. It was her good fortune that this portion of the moon was hidden by the planet's shadow, giving her the chance to first check out what all was being done to temper the riot, and who was involved. To her surprise, there was nothing evident on the outside of the crater walls, which meant the situation was either under control, or being carefully watched from within. She was betting on the latter.

Eyeing the towering mound of dirt before her, Maurra realized the time had come to show herself. She had formulated a vague story about why she was here, but she had to keep it simple. The simpler the story, the easier it would be for the guards and all to believe her. And the easier it would be to remember. Once a suspect got caught convoluting a lie, it would all be over, and the meager trust temporarily earned would vanish.

She patted the tiny pistol she'd holstered to her thigh almost absentmindedly. The pistol was purely for show. Nobody went anywhere without protection. If she appeared at the mines sans any sort of weapon, it would raise suspicion. They'd learn soon enough that she was a psion.

A strong beam of light caught her in its center as she trudged toward the gates. It remained locked on her until she reached the outer perimeter marked by wide crisscrossing stripes blasted into the ground. Maurra continued to walk confidently toward the gates' threshold.

"Halt!"

She slowed and looked up at the top of the crater jutting so high overhead, she had to crane her neck to see the top.

"Halt, intruder!"

Thank the heavens for the translation chip in her arm. But the tone in the voice would have been enough to make her stop in her tracks. It was menacing and filled with unmistakable threat.

Standing inside the warning perimeter, she stared up again at the tops of the crater. This time she noticed the guard boxes with their windows that blended perfectly against the natural rock. *Boy, they must be shitting their pants to see I'm a lone female. Bet they don't get many of us out here.* Earlier communication with the moon would not have given them any sort of clue as to her gender, since the communiqués had to filter through a translator first. As a result, everyone sounded male until personal eye contact was established.

"Halt and prepare to be received!"

Halt and... What the? "I'm already halted, gragholes," she muttered. Nevertheless, she remained where she was until the welcoming committee exited the gates and came to accost her.

Four Ellinod, all in uniforms that vaguely reminded her of Safan's suit the first time she'd seen him, sauntered up to her and stopped within the periphery. They eyed her up and down, noting her sweaty, disheveled appearance and the tiny squirt gun at her side. Immediately they dismissed her as unimportant, if she read their expressions correctly, and that's exactly how she hoped they would see her. Unimportant, and therefore non-threatening.

The Ellinod on the right corner addressed her. "What is your business here?"

Gee. No niceties? No invite in for a drink?

"My ship developed engine trouble," Maurra said. "I'm short on supplies, and I was wondering if I could get a few days' rations to help tide me over until I get her to a base where she can be decently repaired." At least that much was the truth. She gave them her best wide-eyed, helpless expression.

At the mention of her ship, they knew who she was. They even visibly relaxed their stance somewhat. Each one of them was huge and hulking, but there was no comparison to Safan's size. She also noted the heavy-barrel sidearms they carried. Multi-shot phaser pistols. A little voice in the back of her head told her that if these weapons were the best they carried, things were already looking up. Phaser fire was like soft gelatin against her psi powers.

"What's your destination?" the head Ellinod asked.

"Farak Took Mees." It was the first place to pop into her head. It was also a good distance away.

"What's your mission?"

Maurra gave a one-sided shrug. "Merchant ship on the cheap. Right now I'm empty, but I'm on my way to pick up my next cargo."

"Cargo of what?"

She gave him a tired smile. "I'll find out when I get there. With my kind of clientele, I don't ask a lot of questions."

The Ellinod nodded their massive heads. She was what was referred to as a mercenary merchant. Cargo hauled, no questions asked. There were hundreds like her roaming the galaxies.

Maurra shuffled from one foot to the other as she cleared her throat. "I hate to ask again, but would you happen to have a few foodstuffs you can spare? I can pay, but I don't have much. And I really, *really* would appreciate the assistance." She poured on the "semi-helpless female caught in a situation where she could use a friendly gesture" act.

The squad looked around, looking to see if she had an accomplice somewhere. Maurra frowned, tired of the stalling. "Go ahead and scan my ship," she told them. "I'm alone."

She heard something akin to a snort of amusement. The leader motioned toward her weapon. "Is that all you have to protect yourself?"

"On me? Yes. Why?"

"What if you're accosted by pirates?"

She adjusted her stance, crossing her arms over her chest, until she gave them what she hoped would be a cocky attitude. "I'm fast, I'm damn good, and I could beat your butt in under fifteen seconds," she told him in a no-nonsense tone. "Want to try me?"

The remark made them all laugh out loud, but it was enough. She wouldn't have to prove herself, which was good. So far, all was going as she'd hoped it would.

"If we supply you to get you to Ve Onor Targus Four, will that be enough?"

Giving them her best smile, Maurra nodded. There was a decent repair base in that system, and it was between here and her supposed destination.

Waving her in, the Ellinod closed ranks around her, and together they started for the gates.

Chapter Twenty-Seven
Rebellion

Even without turning her head, Maurra was able to get a very good grip on the situation inside the crater. There had to be at least a dozen patrol ships docked inside. Their weapons were pointed at the mine entrance, which was nothing more than a set of immense double doors set inside a pimple-shaped dome in the center of the crater. Apparently administration's solution to subduing the riots was to barricade the inmates inside and either starve them back into complacency, or hope they ended up killing one another. After all, a life sentence was a life sentence, and how the sentence ended was of no concern to them.

In her opinion, both solutions could lead to disaster.

Standing in a semi-circle around the whole thing, an entire platoon of heavily armed troopers stood ready, weapons cradled in their arms or at-ready. Maurra estimated the range between the ships, the troopers, and the entrance, and judged it to be too close. If there should come a blast from the interior of the mines, those men and vehicles would be caught up and destroyed in the outflow. She mentally shook her head at the stupidity.

"Does our layout impress you?"

She stared in surprise at the Ellinod leader. He must have mistaken her reaction as awe. *Might as well play along.*

"Do you always have so many people guarding the mines?"

This time the leader gave her a confused look. "What do you mean?"

They had passed the main core and were heading toward a bank of one-story buildings built into the crater's crown-like spires jutting overhead. Maurra tried to shake off the feeling of something being wrong about the whole situation. Normally, if she had been at one hundred percent, she would have immediately shifted into warning mode, firing up her powers and readying herself against an attack. But she reminded herself that this was a place filled with psychotic and heartless killers, as well as ruthless thugs, brigands, and con artists who were, at the moment, fighting back. Of course she would be inundated with the worse kind of vibes that would set her teeth and her nerves on edge. It was an effort to appear uninformed.

"I've never seen so many weapons in one place."

"Where are you from?" the leader asked. He was suspicious, and rightfully so. Who wasn't already aware of the news regarding the riot?

"Alintarus."

The Ellinod visibly relaxed, as well as the others surrounding her. The little underdeveloped system had established a reputation of its own. And if by chance someone decided to check out her story, it would be easy enough to discover her original port of call.

A high-pitched whine speared her eardrums, bringing tears of pain. Maurra stopped and clutched her ears at the sound. The others also halted and began shaking their heads as the whine became a scream as it gradually grew louder and higher. She felt her powers kicking in as her body instinctively tried to protect itself, and she dropped to her knees, bowing her head toward the white, powdery soil to keep the reddish coil roiling on her forehead from being noticed.

Tucking herself into a near-ball saved her.

The mine's doors exploded outward in a flash of white-hot fire. Percussive waves tossed the closest vehicles backwards, flipping some of them like toys in a high wind, and guards were shredded like thin fabric. Warm blood showered the interior of the crater like rain.

The bomb temporarily deafened her, and for a few moments Maurra was unaware of what had happened until she was picked up and thrown the remaining few meters into the side of the nearest building. Fortunately, her psion powers gave her enough cushion to prevent her from injuring herself. Slightly disoriented, she glanced around to see that the other Ellinod who had been with her hadn't fared as well. All of them were unconscious. A couple had limbs twisted in unnatural angles. Blood was splattered everywhere.

A muted roar drew her attention to the mine's opening as prisoners began to exit, screeching in victory as they ran every which way, brandishing mining tools as makeshift weapons. Many of them stopped to retrieve the guards' weapons as they headed for the pulsar gates.

The few guards who had escaped the initial force of the blast began firing at the oncoming horde, but there were too many prisoners. It took every ounce of willpower for Maurra to remain still and not lend her aid to the guards as she watched the escapees quickly take control of the prison crater.

One Ellinod climbed on top of an overturned speeder and roared at the others. With her ears continuing to ring, Maurra was unable to make out what he was saying, but from his posturing it was clear he was definitely the leader. The others turned away from the gates and began to gather around the vehicle, she guessed to wait for their orders. She never saw or sensed the Ellinod come up from behind her until she was grabbed by the arm and thrown forward. She landed face-first in the dirt, jarred but unhurt.

This wasn't like her. At least, this wasn't the old her, back when she was a JoJo. Had she been wearing the uniform, she would have had no compunction about leaping to her feet and making short shrift of every breathing creature inside the crater. It would have taken her mere seconds to knock them out, but her instincts kept telling her to hold back, to keep her powers hidden until it was the right time, the perfect moment.

Pretend weakness. Pretend helplessness. The time will come soon enough when you can reveal yourself.

"Got another live one!"

He was answered by a shot from overhead. The phaser covered him with a pale pink glow before it vanished and the Ellinod slumped to the ground, unconscious.

The leader growled fiercely and gave an order. Immediately, more than a dozen prisoners disappeared inside various doorways which would lead them up to the guards still stationed in the towers. Maurra barely had time to comprehend everything when another hand grabbed her by the back of the shirt and literally threw her onto her feet.

"Move it!"

A shove at the small of her back was enough to start her stumbling toward the small group of prisoners still gathered around the overturned vehicle that the leader was using as a dais. One of the guards who had greeted her, and managed to survive the blast, was roughly pushed next to her. He hissed in pain as his bloody, twisted arm swung uselessly out of its socket, held only in place by the sleeve. Blood poured down his arms. The creature would soon bleed to death if he wasn't tended to.

They halted next to the damaged patrol skid. Everyone stared up at the Ellinod who stared back down at them. Maurra noted he was also covered in blood and filth. Huge claw tracks ran down the left side of his neck and shoulder, and his left horn bore a large crack. Knowing how sensitive an

Ellinod's horns were, she winced to think of the agony he must have endured — or could still be enduring.

She gave a quick glance around, noting how the rest of the prisoners appeared to have gouged their way up the sides of the mine to escape the horrors below. Their blood- and sweat-soaked clothing was nothing more than rags. They were gaunt, some almost skeletal, and all were covered in sores. Their hollow eyes made their expressions appear maniacal. It was clear they were suffering from dehydration and near starvation, making her wonder how they had found the strength to fight. A sense of dread crawled over her as she realized that the term "life sentence" had a wholly different connotation here than most people realized. For a moment she didn't know whether to congratulate them on accomplishing such a feat by reaching the surface, or worry what their next move would be.

A group of Ellinod exited a doorway leading up into the towers, drawing everyone's attention. "It's clear," one yelled, "but the guard may have notified the landing pad."

The leader disagreed. "Communications were cut prior to blowing the doors."

"Won't the guards at the pad become suspicious when they don't hear from main command?" someone in the crowd asked.

Another Ellinod stepped forward. Maurra got the impression he was the second in command.

"That's what we're hoping. We need someone to open the gates. If we can lure them here and get them to do that, we can get to the landing pad and make our escape from this place."

Several prisoners raised their tool weapons overhead and cheered. Maurra bit her lower lip. Although she was appalled by the treatment these creatures had suffered, in many cases it was a lot more humane than what many of them had put their victims through. She had to keep reminding herself that the majority of those condemned to be here deserved it.

Casually she tried to look around to see if she could spot Safan, but he was not among the group. If he was, he was swallowed up by the masses.

There was no way she could allow these aliens to escape the mines, but she couldn't take them down with her psi powers. Not yet. Not until she found out what had happened to Safan.

What if he was still down in the mines?

What if...

Her throat suddenly closed up, and she felt her skin grow cold and tight.

What if Safan was already dead?

A sense of helplessness spread through her. It was quickly followed by the heat of growing anger. She clenched her teeth. If these creatures had killed Safan, she would have no compunction about blasting them the same way she'd attacked the Kronners. But until someone with the ability to open the pulse gates arrived, she was trapped in here with everyone else. If she took them down now, there was the good chance they'd regain consciousness before reinforcements showed up.

No. First she had to find Safan. After that, she could neutralize the prisoners.

This is, *if* she could find Safan.

"What do we do with them?"

She was jostled and made to move forward slightly, along with the injured guard. A few meters away, two more injured guards were pressed closer to the makeshift dais.

The leader's reply was curt and not surprising. "They're our hostages, just in case."

Just in case. Maurra fully understood what the Ellinod meant. In case the prisoners' plans were foiled when someone came to investigate, she and the others would be used to barter for the escapees' freedom. But there was no doubt in her mind she and the other three guards were totally expendable.

Chapter Twenty-Eight
Discovered

The order went out for the grounds to be cleared. Immediately some of the prisoners began righting the vehicles while others started dragging the dead into the offices lining the inner crater ring. The injured were also removed and placed in a separate set of offices. Maurra watched as two Ellinod picked up body parts and stacked them in their arms. *All fine and dandy, guys, but how are you going to cover up all the blood before the cavalry arrives?*

One of the prisoners shoved a phaser gun into the guard behind her, who in turn bumped into her. "Move!"

He pushed at them again to herd them in the direction toward the gates and the towers bracing them on either side. Which meant that if the authorities coming to investigate failed to open the huge doors, she and the guards could be put on public display and probably murdered one at a time until the prisoners' demands were granted.

As soon as the mine had blown, the entire crater had gone on lockdown. The only way the prisoners could escape off this rock was to make it over to the landing pad and confiscate the ships. But in order to do that, they first had to get through those immense gates. She glanced up at the smooth vertical walls surrounding them. There was no way anyone could climb out of this place.

Maurra bit her lower lip and glanced at the other three guards, then judged her inner strength. If they huddled close enough to her, she was certain she could shield them when she blasted the prisoners. If she couldn't save Safan, then the least she could do would be to rescue the remaining guards.

They shuffled past the center core of the mine shaft where prisoners were trying to disguise the lack of doors on the entrance with one of the vehicles. A small handful of prisoners was shoving the land speeders around to hide the scorch marks from the explosion when her psionic powers alerted her. She frowned as she stumbled over the large rock fragments. It wasn't so much as a danger signal as it was...

She looked up and over at the group of Ellinod. They were busy trying to turn a speeder right side up, except for one. One with a peculiarly crooked horn. One who turned around and stood frozen to stare at her in shock and disbelief. He wasn't as wasted away as the others, considering the short amount of time he had been here, but the dark bruises and half-healed welts across his chest and face were evidence of how bad things were in the mines.

Maurra felt her heart slamming against her ribcage.

Safan!

He started toward her but she quickly signaled him to stay, making a hand gesture they had used when aboard the Kronner ship. *Wait.*

Another prisoner growled something at him, and he reluctantly turned to lend a hand, but she could sense him keeping her in his sight. He understood she was planning something. He trusted her.

Her group continued toward the gates where the leader was standing with several others. The Ellinod eyed her and the injured guards before bringing his attention back to her.

"Who are you?"

"Teana Amiattro. If you've got the cargo, I've got the price. Who are you?" she shot back. It wasn't hard to feign her rising anger or fear at what was occurring.

The leader ignored her retort. "What are you doing here?"

"I developed engine trouble. This place gave me clearance to land—"

"Hold it!" The leader reached out and almost poked her in the chest with a swollen finger bearing a broken claw. Maurra immediately leaned back to prevent contact. If he touched her, there would be no way she could prevent her psi core from throwing a defensive net around her for protection. And if that had happened, her secret would be out. To the majority of these creatures, the only good JoJo would be a dead one.

The leader didn't seem to notice her avoidance. He gaped at her in happy disbelief.

"You have a ship here?"

Maurra nodded toward the gates. "Actually it's out there, a few hundred meters from the main landing pad. On the dark side of the moon." She didn't ask him why the sudden interest. She already knew. It would be one more conveyance away from this place.

"Will it fly?"

She gave him a half shrug. "Depends. You got someone here who knows his way around a Tygrecian low boy?"

The leader thought about it. Glancing over her head, he stared at the flock of prisoners working in the background. He motioned for a few to join them. To Maurra's surprise, one of them was Safan. Either that, or he had attached himself to the ones ordered over.

"We're in luck. There's a merchant vessel downed on the other side of the landing pad. That gives us another ship. But it's developed engine problems. Any of you know someone who's familiar with Tygrecian ships?"

"I've driven one," Safan said in a gritty voice.

"Good enough." Turning back to Maurra, the leader smiled. The sight of it turned her stomach. "That gives us one more hostage to kill if they refuse to open the gates."

Maurra shot a look at Safan. He glared at her, undeniably angry. For the hundredth time she wished she could read minds. What was he thinking? More importantly, what was he planning?

He's looking at me like he hates me.

With the force of a bomb going off inside her, the bitter, ugly truth sucked every bit of breath and strength from her, and her legs went out from under her. The leader laughed maliciously as she sank onto the dirt in shock.

Yeah, go ahead and laugh, you girg fucker. You think I'm reacting to your little speech because you no longer need me, now that you have a fellow prisoner who can man the controls of my ship.

But the heart sickening reality was that she finally realized she had been hanging her emotions on a dead star. She had developed feelings for the Ellinod that weren't going to be reciprocated. He didn't care for her. He never had. The tenderness and gentleness she had sensed in him had been real, but they weren't deep. They had been only for the moment when he'd needed to take her, to prevent them both from being annihilated. His feelings weren't permanent. They weren't from his heart or his soul. They weren't...

Oh, by the freaking heavens, Maurra! What have you done? What have you been telling yourself? That you're in love with him? He's an Ellinod, you idiot! What were you expecting? For him to suddenly open his arms to you? To come charging over to keep you safe the moment he saw you? Did you honestly believe that this creature would develop feelings for you? If you did, then you're the biggest fool in the galaxy. And all of this was for naught. All of your planning has been nothing but foolhardy and worthless, you stupid, stupid woman!

Well, maybe not worthless. She could still pull a good deed or two out of this confusing mess. Once the reinforcements arrived, she could take down the prisoners and rescue the surviving guards.

Wiping the tears from her cheeks, she got back up and faced the leader who had moved away to talk to another one of his minions. They were too far away for her translator to catch, but it wasn't necessary now. She knew their plans.

Backing up carefully, keeping her movements discreet, Maurra rejoined the injured guards. Bowing her head, she leaned in and whispered, "On my word, grab hold of me, any part of me, and hold on. Don't let go. Do you understand?"

Three soft grunts answered her. One ventured a question. "Why?"

"I'm a psion."

Their reactions didn't surprise her. Maybe at some point they'd hoped the psi corps would infiltrate their ranks anyway, regardless of the rhetoric being spouted about non-interference. Either way, they remained huddled close to where they could grab her at a moment's notice.

Maurra sniffed, wiped away the last of the useless tears, and raised her face. Immediately her eyes locked onto green ones less than two meters away. The look on his face told her everything. He had overheard her instructions to the guards. He knew what she planned to do.

She reached out with her sensors but detected nothing from him. No trepidation, no anger. Nothing.

Now that you know, Safan, what are you going to do about it?

A cry went out from behind them. Many of the prisoners started scurrying for the doorways. Others concealed themselves behind the vehicles, out of sight from anyone standing at the gates. An Ellinod prisoner carrying a mining rock cutter shoved the sharpened end into one guard's back. "Move."

"I thought you were going to use us as hostages to get them to open the gates," Maurra spat at him as they hobbled toward one of the gate's towers where the leader and two of his men had already disappeared through an open door.

"We are," the prisoner half-growled, half-laughed. "We have other plans for you first."

Maurra gave the creature a perplexed look, but it was more of an excuse to search behind them to see where Safan had gone. It was with no surprise she found him trailing along directly behind their captors.

After all, he needed to let his leader know what he'd discovered.

Chapter Twenty-Nine
Hope

They were nearly at the door when they heard the sound of patrol land speeders approaching. "Move it!" The prisoner jabbed at them to make them hurry. Instead, the injured guard beside Maurra fell to his knees. She whirled on the Ellinod in anger.

"He's injured, you prick! He can't move that fast!"

Safan came up from behind and pointed to a tall column of limestone to their left. "Over there. They can't see us from the gates if we hide over there," he suggested.

"Over there" was a narrow but deep indentation in the column. The prisoner continued to jab at the guards, forcing them to cram inside. Maurra angled her body enough to where she ended up facing outward with the three creatures behind her, sheltering them. It turned out better than she expected. This way the guards would be within her protective shield without the need for them to hold onto her.

The prisoner turned to Safan. "Now what?"

"Now I relieve you of your duty," Safan calmly answered, and dealt the prisoner a heavy-fisted blow to the side of the creature's face. The prisoner sank to the ground without a sound as Safan grabbed his weapon.

Maurra stared at him in confusion as he shoved the creature inside a small fissure in the rock wall. When he was done, he hefted the mining instrument and pressed inside the crack with them while also keeping an eye on what was happening at the gates.

This close to him, she could smell the stench of the mines upon him, and for a moment her heart went out to him before she managed to close it back up in its own little cell. "What are you doing?" she whispered.

He glanced back at her, and his eyes darted up to her forehead. At this point, the sign of her power coalescing on her face was no longer an issue.

"Do you really have a ship nearby?" he murmured back.

"What do you think?"

"How long do you think it'll take to get the engines fixed? Are they completely shot?"

"What do you care?" she answered, already seeing where this was going.

They could hear the patrol speeders pulling up to the gates just as another ship flew over the crater. This would all be over in a few minutes, she realized, once the pilot caught sight of the destroyed mine doors, the puddles of blood, and the prisoners trying to hide behind the damaged vehicles.

Someone tried to bring down the craft with a pulse gun, not knowing the phaser blasts were useless against the ship's metal hull. A moment later, a loud voice was projected from the gates.

"We know you've managed to seize the inner compound. Give up now, and you'll be given food and medical care. Resist, and we will wipe out the interior with a proton bomb. You have fifty microns to reply."

Safan made a move to go forward when Maurra grabbed his shoulder. "What are you doing?"

"I'm going to tell them about the injured guards."

"And get yourself killed!"

"Not if I go out there empty-handed," he argued, dropping the tool onto the dirt.

"I don't mean by the guards," Maurra told him. "By the other prisoners! Or have you forgotten they're armed, too?"

His eyes bore into hers, and she got the impression he was searching for something. Waiting for her. "What do you care?" he finally asked.

She answered before she thought. "Why the fuck do you think I came here in the first place?"

His eyes filled with hope. She sensed it, along with relief and...

Her heart emerged from its cage. His open and raw emotions were too much for her to handle at this moment, but they were what she had been praying to see.

Caring. Concern. And...affection.

Taking a deep, shuddering breath, Maurra whispered, "I came to save you, you idiot. My engines are fine. My ship is fine. I just pretended —"

"Twenty microns!"

"Look, you stay here," she told him. "Let me go out. My shield will protect me. You know that." She could feel her powers flowing through her, tensing her muscles and tingling her nerve endings. At this point her gift would be visible as a nearly solid ball of reddish flame.

"You."

The soft voice drew their attention to the guard holding his shattered arm.

"Now I recognize you. You were the ones the Kronners held captive," he gasped.

"I don't know what you're talking about," Maurra snapped at him and turned back around. "All right. It's show time."

"Maurra." Safan snagged her arm. "If you take down the prisoners like I think you're planning on doing, then you'll have to take me down with them."

"You're coming with me."

"I can't follow you. And if you leave me untouched, they will kill me the second they get the chance." His warm hand brushed against her belly. "You have to take me out."

"No way. Just stay here and keep your eyes and ears open. Then take the first opening you see, all right? But while I'm firing, you stay back and out of sight, you got me? Stay out of my line of sight!"

They remained staring at each other another moment or two, studying each other's faces, waiting to see who would make the first move, the first gesture. In the end, it was Safan who let go of her arm and stepped back. Maurra nodded and moved away from the hideaway, out into the open where she could see the entire interior of the crater, and where both the prisoners and guards could see her.

Chapter Thirty
Debt

She couldn't give the prisoners time to react. Lifting her arms overhead, Maurra aimed her powers in one large blanket of crimson light. Because her ability was mental, she needed to make direct, visual contact with her target. Thus, the prisoners inside the towers or hiding behind the damaged vehicles were untouched until they popped their heads up to aim and fire their weapons. The moment they did, their bodies went rigid.

She sent a sensor web over the interior as she kept her back to the gates. Wherever she detected a figure, she bathed that section until the prisoner showed himself. She knew that eventually they all would. It was one of the quirks of every living species. At some point curiosity would make them try to take a peek at her, or at least look to see how things were faring. And when they did, a bright red neuron-freezing beam would take them down.

She wished she could see the guards' expressions, but her concentration couldn't be jeopardized. It was difficult enough to keep her powers contained within the narrowed field of the crater. If she'd had her JoJo gun, she could focus the reddish wash with greater ease, intensity, and direction.

This was the first time she had used her ability since recovering, and it felt damn good. No, screw that. It felt fantastic! This was what she had been created to do. This was her job, her calling, her destiny, JoJo or not. There was no greater sense of accomplishment than to help and protect those who needed it, and to take down those who were determined to cause misery.

Someone in one of the towers tried to fire on her with a phaser gun. Maurra narrowed her eyes, and a single thought dropped the sniper cold. With the Ellinod down, she no longer sensed anything before her. Gradually, she reduced her power until it was no more than two gyroscoping semi-transparent orbs enveloping her hands. Turning around, she looked out at the guards hovering behind the gates.

"It's done. You can come in safely now."

She watched the lights around the gates dim and fade away, and the land speeders slowly pulled into the main area. One vehicle bearing the crest of the prison warden stopped near her, and a large Ellinod wearing a bright gold vest got out. He gave the area a quick once-over, then walked over to where she stood with her hands still extended. She didn't want to shut down. Not yet. Not until she was satisfied the situation was stable.

The warden came right to the point. "You're a JoJo?" He glanced down at her lack of uniform for emphasis.

"No."

"You're a psion."

"Yes, but not all of us are JoJos."

His eyes narrowed. She watched, waiting, knowing that sooner or later it would come to him. Revelation came sooner.

"You were the JoJo captured by the Kronners," he flatly stated. Before she could reply, he added, "Why are you here?" Again, she didn't have the chance to answer when he did. "The Orgoran you were with was sentenced here." The Ellinod nodded his head. "It all makes sense now. You came to help him escape."

Maurra knew when it was time for honesty. Any lie she told now would not help her or Safan, and could actually make matters worse. "Yes." The one simple word was enough.

"Where is he?"

Maurra threw a thumb over her shoulder. "There's a small crevasse in the rock near the gates. He's watching over three injured guards and waiting for my signal."

"There were survivors?"

"Just the three, as far as we know. I don't know how the prisoners managed to blow the doors, or how many more are still down in the mines."

"We'll do a quick head count. Were you here during the initial riots?"

"No," Maurra hurried to tell him.

"So it was happenstance that you came to help free him when the riots took place?"

Time for more honesty. "Not quite. When I found out about the riots, I came to take advantage of the confusion. It was happenstance I was here when the prisoners blew the mine doors."

"Yet you stayed. After the prisoners escaped, you stayed to help when you and the Orgoran could have already made your way off-planet by the time we arrived."

She opened her mouth to reply when she realized he was right. She had the power to take Safan and herself away from this place, and leave the prisoners and guards to fight it out to the bitter end. But instead she had remained to help bring about an end to the conflict.

The Ellinod studied her thoughtfully. Maurra tried to see if she could read him. Instead she felt a thread of trepidation, and turned to see Safan emerge from hiding, carrying one of the injured guards. He remained weaponless, but two replacement guards followed closely behind while two others went to retrieve the other injured Ellinod.

Linda Mooney

She watched as Safan was led over to where the guards were dumping the unconscious prisoners in the center of the crater. More guards converged on the mine entrance where several began jury-rigging harnesses to take them down into the tunnels. One guard bearing crests on his epaulettes ran over to get orders from the warden, who had been joined by what Maurra assumed was a physician.

Since the Ellinod had momentarily forgotten her, Maurra drew her power back into herself and turned around in time to see an armed guard order Safan to place the injured Ellinod into one of the land speeders. Once Safan had obeyed, the guard gave him another order. Safan turned, spotted her, and paused. Without warning, the guard whipped his weapon around and punched Safan twice, once in the side of the face, followed by a hard blow to the chest. Punishment for not obeying quickly enough.

Maurra screamed and bolted toward him as he fell to his knees, but she underestimated Safan's strength and endurance. He grabbed the guard's gun and wrenched it from the Ellinod's grasp. The guard stumbled, pulling out another smaller pistol to aim at Safan.

She acted without thinking, sending a bolt of pure energy at the guard, who went stiff. The pistol fell from unfeeling fingers, and the Ellinod toppled over like a rock. Within seconds the entire force went on alert, and every gun turned on her and Safan. Pivoting, Maurra opened herself once more, relief making her stronger when she felt Safan's hand at the small of her back.

"Call off your guards!" she yelled. "Drop your weapons, or I'll drop you!"

The warden motioned for the guards to step down and stared at her for a long moment. "Don't be stupid, psion. The Ellinod is a convicted criminal. He belongs here. You don't, so you're free to leave."

"I'm not leaving without him."

171

The stand-off might have continued when she spotted the door to the tower at the far end of the crater suddenly swing open. The leader of the revolt and his men exited where they had been hiding. With weapons firing, they sent most of the replacement guards and the warden diving for cover as they tried to shoot back. Maurra noticed the Ellinod were heading straight for the gates, which had not been turned back on. Throwing back her arms, she gathered her power into one enormous band of psion energy and launched the glowing ribbon at the escapees. Watching the half-dozen prisoners get overtaken by the blood-red field was a particularly satisfying moment for her.

The glow had barely faded away when the warden straightened from where he'd been crouching behind his patrol vehicle and yelled for the gates to be turned back on, in the event another prisoner untouched by Maurra's power tried to make a break for it. Once he was certain order had been restored, the warden looked around and motioned toward the craft. "Let's talk in here. Bring the Orgoran with you."

Maurra stepped down her psychic energy. Behind her, Safan slowly lowered the guard's weapon to leave it on the ground. Together they approached the vehicle with the warden already seated in front. They climbed inside, and the doors sealed shut. The warden got straight to the point.

"I owe you a huge debt," he told her. "I could have lost a lot more guards, not counting the ones you saved earlier." Nodding at Safan, he added, "From what I've seen, Orgoran, you don't belong here either, but I can't negate what our laws have decreed."

"And I won't let Safan stay here and rot," Maurra told him.

"I believe you, and unfortunately for me, you have the ability to back your words." He glanced out the front viewscreen at the armed squadron of guards watching and waiting with weapons primed. Well-trained men who would not hesitate to shoot at his signal, or if they believed he couldn't give them one. "If you're willing to trust me, I have an idea."

Maurra looked over at Safan who gave her a nod. "We're listening."

Chapter Thirty-One
Freedom

The warden started up the craft and slowly drove the land speeder past his armed guards, past the unconscious figures of the stunned prisoners, and up to the pulsar gates. Punching in a code in the ship's computer shut off the force field beams, allowing him to glide out of the crater. As soon as they were clear, he reinstated the gates.

"Listen carefully because there won't be time to repeat anything," he said, sending the speeder into high gear. "This is the story. You've taken me hostage, but you promised nothing would happen to me as long as I took you straight to the landing pad and dropped you off there." He paused to swallow, and Maurra realized he was more nervous than he appeared. "I take it your ship is nearby?"

"It's some distance away from the landing pad, on the dark side," she said. "I feigned engine trouble, so I was instructed to land there in case they blew."

The warden nodded. "As soon as I send a signal, my men will converge on this ship. You'll have to jump before then."

"Got it."

"By the way, how long will those prisoners be out?"

"Eighty microns. Maybe more, maybe less. Depends on each one's stamina and physical health."

"You understand why I'm doing this, don't you?" the warden asked. He never took his eyes off the controls or from the viewscreen. A flashing light on his communications console gave evidence that his squadron was trying to reach him. The longer he remained incommunicado, the more feasible the story of him being a hostage would appear.

"Some," Maurra replied.

"I have a wife and two children. I have sixteen more orbits before my time is up on this rock, and I can take a safer and more comfortable position back on my home world. You saved me back there. You saved my guards. And although I don't condone what you and the Orgoran did, I count myself among the many who believe you had no choice but to obey the Kronners, or die."

"They told us we should have died," Safan growled, finally speaking up. "They told us our lives meant nothing if we broke the very laws we were supposed to uphold."

"It is the way of our world," the warden concurred. "If those of us who are stanchions of the law break the very rules we make everyone else abide by, then we are worse offenders than they are. Therefore our punishment should be greater, to prove to the populace that we take our jobs and our duties very seriously."

"That's crat shit and you know it," Maurra hissed. "Your laws are no different than the laws I gave my word to uphold. But all of those laws, *all* of them, were created to prevent people and creatures like us from *voluntarily* choosing to break them. Nowhere is it taken into account that someone may force another to break the rules. To me, that makes Safan and me victims, not criminals."

The warden chanced a glance sideways at her. "That is exactly why I will give you this one chance. Use it wisely, and don't ever venture back to this quadrant of space again. When a prisoner is given life, it means life."

They drew nearer to the landing area, close enough to see the individual buildings, the living quarters and offices, and the large warehouses and hangars where some of the ships docked overnight. Two smaller flyjets raced past them to land at the pad and disgorged several armed guards, who took a stance at the end of the pad to await the warden's arrival. A welcoming committee, Maurra realized grimly.

"You know they won't hesitate to kill you, too, don't you?" she asked the warden.

"I know that. Are you ready to jump ship? As soon as you're gone, I'll continue on all the way to the pad where I'll make a full report."

"As soon as you land, your guards will come after us," Safan observed.

"Then you had better run as fast as you can, and hope you reach your ship before they reach you."

Maurra stared at the landscape growing larger in the viewscreen. "What if I blast them?"

"There's too many of them, and they'll be coming at you from all directions."

"Then you don't know psions."

The warden shrugged. "Maybe not, but why make things worse than they already are? Run for it, psion, and take the Orgoran with you. Find another solar system or another galaxy, but leave this one. Find a new home, and create new identities, and live the rest of your lives as escapees."

"But it will be a life," Safan said. "And it will be a longer one than what I would have had in the mines."

Maurra looked over to see the Ellinod staring at her. They had a lot to talk about, but it would have to wait.

The warden made some adjustments at the console, then gestured toward the back of the ship. "There's a rear exit door. Keep down to stay below the engines. Are you ready?"

Maurra launched herself over the back seats to where a narrow cargo hatch was located. Safan pressed up behind her, ready to follow her out the moment she jumped. At the sound of the latch clicking, Maurra shoved the door upward and together they leaped as one.

The warden had maneuvered the land speeder as close to the moon's surface as he could manage at the speed he was traveling. In spite of that, hitting the packed dirt knocked the breath from them as they tumbled and rolled for several meters. Maurra gasped for air as she got to her knees and crawled over to where Safan had ended up on his stomach. Managing to stand on unsteady legs, she grabbed his arm to help his to his feet. Safan jerked away from her grasp.

"I can manage. Go! *Go!*" he growled.

Maurra took a quick look in the distance at the warden's land speeder. She could see the rear engines flaring as it was getting ready to land. Whirling around, she stared at the dark, barren horizon and tried to remember where she'd left the cruiser.

"Maurra, which way's the ship?"

"I'm trying to get my bearings, damn it!" They were close. She would swear they were. But the guards would soon be on them if they didn't take off running *now*. "Which way?" Oh, dearest gods, *which way?*

Struggling to remember, she bent over and clasped her knees to clear her head when she felt something pinch the sensitive flesh above her right ribcage.

The remote.

Reaching under her blouse, she peeled the little cylinder from underneath her breast and stared at it for a split second. "Lorri, can you hear me? Lorri! Lorri, I need your coordinates and a pickup up *now!*"

Miraculously, a tiny voice answered, "On my way, Captain!"

"I'll meet you in the middle! Show me where to go!"

In answer, a small flare burst like a yellow incandescent sun on the horizon to their right. She and Safan took off toward it, running as fast as they could, although Maurra could tell the Ellinod was no longer in peak physical shape. He may have only spent a couple of weeks in that pit, but it had been long enough to already leave its mark. He was tiring quickly. She slowed a hair to keep even with him when he shot her an angry look.

"If it means leaving me behind, save yourself, Maurra."

"Shut up and run, Orgoran!"

Another glance over her shoulder spotted several patrol craft racing toward them. They were gaining, and gaining fast. If there was one thing to be grateful for, it was the fact that the guards wouldn't shoot at them until they were close enough to ensure a direct hit.

"*Lorri, move your ass!*"

"I'm hurrying," the craft replied calmly. "Where shall I land?"

"Fuck the landing! Come along beside us and lower a ladder!"

"Very well, Captain."

Her legs felt like they were wearing lead weights. Her lungs were on fire, and her whole body ached. She could not imagine how the Ellinod was faring, but it had to be many times worse. Once he stumbled, almost falling over his own bare feet, but he managed to right himself in time. His face was a sickly shade of gray, and sweat was rolling off of him. He was struggling for air so loudly, she could barely hear the sounds of the patrol cruisers drawing nearer.

The little ship swooped down from overhead, startling them at its sudden appearance. As instructed, it dropped its short landing ladder and kept pace with them as Maurra leaped for the handrail. Pivoting around, she wrapped one leg over a support strut and bent down to offer both hands. Safan reached for her, stumbled again, and lost ground.

"Haul it, Safan! Lorri!"

"Adjusting," the ship said.

This time she managed to grab the remnants of his shirt at the shoulders. The abused fabric ripped loudly as two enormous hands grasped her upper arms. Maurra let the ship's momentum help swing him onto the ladder and up into the hold with her. For a few seconds they stood clutching each other and gasping for breath as the ship sealed its hull.

"Captain, you're being hailed by the committee following us. Shall I respond?"

Maurra raised her face from where she had been resting her forehead on the Ellinod's chest. The sound of his rapid heartbeat reminded her of the first time she had listened to its rhythm. Looking up, she saw the creature staring at her with an unfathomable expression on his face.

"Captain?"

"No. No, don't answer. Just get us the fuck out of here."

"Coordinates?"

"I don't care. Out of this galaxy. Out of this system. Anywhere that's safe. Any suggestions?"

"Well, the Peldinar system is three chrono days from here. Vias Daruggah has a large merchant shipyard—"

"And supplies, and anything else we may need. Sounds good, Lorri. Set a course for the Peldinar system, and Vias Daruggah."

"And then what?" Safan finally whispered, breaking his silence. "What do we do now, Maurra?"

"I have a plan."

A brow ridge rose in query above green eyes. "Oh?"

"Yeah. We're going after that son of a treegrit slime slug who orchestrated our kidnapping."

The Ellinod smiled, chuckling softly. "And when we catch him, then what?"

Maurra smiled back. Like her, he had no doubt they would find Tramer Vol Brod. "Then? I don't know. I haven't thought that far ahead. Why? Got any ideas?"

"Yeah, but not regarding Vol Brod," Safan replied, and leaned over to kiss her.

Chapter Thirty-Two
Honesty

Compared to kisses she had received in the past, it was the sweetest, softest kiss she had ever felt. He wasn't an expert in the art, but his lips were firm, and they didn't touch hers as much as they elicited her response to kiss him back. She found herself holding her breath, enthralled by his gentle yet passionate mouth.

He was kissing her. He had instigated it. The wonder of it blinded her, and left her unable to think.

Maurra reached up with one hand to cup the side of his face when she felt something warm and sticky. Her immediate reaction was that the substance wasn't sweat. Drawing back slightly, she looked at her hand. Just as she thought—blood. Upon further examination, she noticed another trickle rolling down his temple and through her handprint. Another stab of guilt struck her.

"You're hurt. You're bleeding above the ear. Are you in pain?"

"I can't hear from that side," he admitted.

"Come inside." She tugged on his arm. "Let me medicate that."

Maurra led him into the small living quarters of the ship. With the Ellinod there, the area appeared smaller and more cramped. Safan collapsed in the command chair and watched as she searched the lockers in the galley for the small medical kit she had uncovered earlier.

"Is there anything to eat?"

She glanced at him over her shoulder. Damn. She should have thought of his other needs. She wasn't accustomed to having a partner, or having to take care of anyone else but herself.

Having a partner. Guess I'm gonna have to get used to it.

Maurra's eyes widened as the idea sunk in. After all these years, did she want to continue going solo? Or was her decision to rescue Safan actually her subconscious confessing her need for more constant companionship?

Companionship? Or companionship meaning Safan?

She tossed several ration packets into his lap. "Enjoy. It's all we have until we can restock somewhere."

Safan ripped open a packet and stuffed the yellow bruulu into his mouth. "Got any creds?" he managed to ask around his chewing.

Maurra shook her head. "I'm flat broke. I used all that I had to buy this ship. The Jora claimed my banking account, along with everything else I owned, when they kicked me off the force. The only things they couldn't take were my personal, non-JoJo related things. I was left with what creds I had on hand."

The cut wasn't deep, but Maurra knew head wounds tended to bleed profusely. She quickly cleaned the spot and applied a cooling, numbing medicant. A protective sealant sprayed over the area further protected it. After putting up the kit, she brought him another handful of food ration packets and a couple of liquids. Safan devoured the contents as she walked up to the bridge console to check the navigational grid.

It would take them three days to reach Vias Daruggah. Three days, unless she redirected the ship to take them elsewhere. But they needed supplies *now*. And by the time they arrived on Vias Daruggah, they'd need fuel. Unfortunately, supplies and fuel took creds, which they were also fresh out of.

Maurra bit her lip. It was hard to think straight. She was wrung out from using her power on Bansheer, and hadn't had the chance to rest and build her strength back up.

"What are you thinking?"

Maurra answered without turning around to face him. "I'm wondering how we're going to restock our supplies."

"How's your fuel?"

She looked back down at the console. "We have enough to get us to Vias Daruggah. After that, it's get out and push time."

"Then we need to figure out a way to earn enough creds so we can restock and refuel before we track down Vol Brod." He belched softly. Maurra turned to see him slowly get to his feet. Pain reflected on his face, reminding her of the conditions he'd been forced to endure inside the mines.

"You need to rest," she urged him.

Safan shook his head. "I need to get rid of the stench of the mines first. I take it this bucket has a cleansing stall?"

"In the back corner."

He started for the rear of the ship, but paused. "Where did you put the medical kit?"

"Would you like me to dress the rest of your wounds?" she offered.

"If you don't mind." He limped off toward the rear.

With every passing minute Maurra could see the Ellinod weakening, lowering his guard and finally allowing himself to relax and heal. More importantly, he totally trusted her. The realization was like a bright halo shining around her. In the past other people had trusted her, but it was more along the lines of them trusting her to do her job. To get whatever needed to be done done, and make the bad guys pay for their crimes. This was a completely different trust she sensed from

Safan, and she discovered she rather liked the warm sensations she got from it.

Maurra took one last look at the navigation panel. Safan had the right idea. A good cleaning, some food, and lots of rest would make a world of difference in her physical and mental abilities. Hers and Safan's.

Going to the rear of the ship, she sat on the floor since she couldn't open the bed until Safan was finished. She was removing her boots when the cleansing chamber stopped humming. Safan stepped out.

Her first reaction was that she'd forgotten how large the Ellinod's genitals were. Dragging her eyes away from the impressive dick, she was startled to see the ugly black and purple splotches across his chest, arms, and legs that turned her stomach. There were also some unidentifiable claw marks, and a couple of suspicious puncture wounds. Fresh blood oozed afresh from several deep scratches. She was unaware she'd gotten to her feet and was approaching him until he grabbed her by the wrist to stop her from touching the wide bruise across his ribs.

"Oh, dear gods, Safan!" Her throat closed up, and she felt the now familiar flush of heat leap into her face, along with the burn of tears in her eyes. "I had no idea."

"They'll heal," he softly said.

She pulled back her hand. "What about the rest of you?" She walked around to look at his back, and was sorry she did. He had been whipped to the point where the flesh had been torn and nearly flayed from his body. It was healing in ragged and sometimes overlapping strips. Impulsively, she pressed a kiss to a small patch of wound-less skin next to his shoulder blade. And another. And another. With the morbid scent of the mines no longer covering him, he once again had that wild, earthy aroma. Musky and masculine. She nuzzled his shoulder.

"Maurra."

Lifting her face, she waited for him to turn around.

"We need rest," Safan told her softly. He cupped her face the same way she had earlier, except his huge hand easily held the entire side of her head.

She gave a nod, and he withdrew his hand, but not before letting his fingers weave through her hair, letting the long reddish locks fall away. "Let me put something on the worst of these first," she requested.

Safan sat on the floor, where she could easily reach the areas needing medication. Once she was satisfied the ugliest wounds had been treated and sealed, she ordered the ship to open the bed.

The floor slid away without the ship responding. Maurra dropped down onto the covers. Safan followed, moving over to avoid taking up the majority of the bed. They settled into comfortable positions as the lights dimmed.

Maurra immediately felt her body sagging. Her eyes drooped, and lassitude turned her muscles into water. She had no idea she was still this exhausted.

The last thing she remembered was Safan rolling over, wrapping his arm around her waist, and pulling her up against him, the way he had done on the Kronner ship. With the heat of his body blanketing her, Maurra fell into deep sleep.

Chapter Thirty-Three
Possession

His hand was hot on her breast. Slowly, the palm rotated her nipple, making it grow taut and sending searing desire between her legs. Maurra carefully arched her back until she rested her head against his chest. His huge hand reached across to her other breast, until his fingers captured the other nipple and gently pinched it.

A moan vibrated in her throat. He was being cautious, tentative in his touch, almost fearful, and she understood why he was being reticent. Except for his hand, the rest of his body remained distant, nothing more than a warm presence at her back. Her next move would mean everything for their future.

Their future together.

Slowly, Maurra rolled over. Her eyes had adjusted to the pale lights coming from the living area above them. Despite the shadows, she could see his questioning gaze locked onto her face. Would she accept him? Or would she reject him? Was her coming to the mines to get him because of something they had yet to admit to each other? Or was there another intent?

Slowly, she plucked the hand touching her breasts and lifted it to her lips. After placing a soft kiss on his fingers, Maurra lowered it to her already wet mound and parted her legs for him.

It was all she needed to do.

It was all he needed to know.

Safan growled as he rose over her and grabbed her hips. A quick twist, and Maurra found herself flipped onto her stomach. Sitting on his knees, he pulled her back toward him and lifted her buttocks. A glance between her legs revealed his erection jutting directly toward her, swinging long and ponderously as it lightly grazed her abdomen. A single drop glittered at its tip, showing he was as ready as she was.

He bent over to reach between her thighs. Long claws lightly trailed across her belly, leaving her shivering with want and anticipation. Maurra peered back over her shoulder to see his attention was focused on her rear. Safan placed a hand on her thigh to steady her. The other hand he used to guide his thickness to her entrance. Pulling back the foreskin, he set the tip against the glistening opening and steadily began to push.

Maurra bowed her head as she fought the frightening sense of taking his enormous size. Like it had the first time, her body tried to prevent him. Then it tried to expel him.

Steady, girl. Take a deep breath and remember how fucking wonderful it felt. This is why you came back for him, isn't it? Because you wanted him to take you again. Because you needed to feel the kind of sexual high only he has been able to give you.

"Yes, yes!" she barely breathed aloud. That was exactly the reason why she'd gone to him. But there was another reason. A reason she didn't dare think about, or even mention, much less admit to herself.

Closing her eyes, she tried to mentally help ease his way inside her.

His erection continued to burrow into her slowly, inexorably. Giving her time to stretch. Giving her time to remember how she was able to accept him, to swallow him.

Maurra felt her whole body tremble with expectation as she waited, wondering what he would do next. She never expected the Ellinod to arch himself over her, releasing her thigh to grasp a breast with each hand. Or for his mouth to close over the juncture between her neck and shoulder. She could feel his teeth clamp down over her flesh, but they didn't puncture it. It was like being placed in a vise and sealed into it painlessly yet effectively.

Without hesitating, Safan started pressing harder into her, entering without pulling back. Drilling her a centimeter at a time until her body finally convulsed. Immediately he paused, and that's when the little vibrations went through her, teasing and rippling, and sending minute shockwaves under her skin. Vibrations she remembered from that time in the cell. Vibrations that had sent her spiraling into a wild, orgasmic frenzy.

Her body poured more wetness through her channel as it tried to expand, to accept his length and girth. She could hear him breathing more heavily, and she felt the heat of every expelled breath across her shoulders. But his teeth remained locked in place, unrelenting but without hurting her.

His hands released her breasts to glide over her belly until they reached her mound. Once they reached her swollen lower lips, Safan placed his fingers on her turgid clit and carefully pinched it.

Her reaction was immediate. Her whole body jerked from the pleasure piercing her. At the same time, Safan sank a little deeper into her while the vibrations continued.

This was nothing like the way it had been when they had been forced to copulate in the cells. This was totally different. Different position, different method...different reaction.

Let go, Maurra. Let yourself go. Give yourself to him. Give all of yourself to him.

It was something she had never done before in her life—allowing herself to lose all control. She had always been the dominant one, the person calling all the shots, even in bed.

But not anymore. She would never be totally in control anymore as long as Safan was her lover. And for some unexplainable reason, Maurra knew she would never have another lover after him.

Let him overcome you, Maurra. Let him have full control. Control of your body as well as your heart and mind. Let him have it, and discover how much ecstasy you can find in his lovemaking.

Suddenly, without warning, he lifted her until her back was arched and she was balanced solely on her knees. Without thinking, Maurra clasped his hands that had returned to her breasts. She gasped as Safan removed his mouth from her neck.

"I take you," he growled close to her ear. "I take you as mine."

Her head swam. Was he making a confession? Or demanding an answer?

"My people do not fornicate without intent," he whispered. "It is our way, and always will be. Back in the cell, my intent was merely survival. But here, here now with you, my intent is possession. Pure and simple, I possess you. I take you as mine, Maurra. What say you? I need your answer if we are to complete ourselves."

Maurra froze. She had heard stories about how the Ellinod took their mates in what was rumored to be a bestial way. Mounting them. Taking them savagely.

She would be his mate, but she already knew her soul and his were bonded. Her womb clenched in anticipation.

His huge erection continued to sink into her a bit at a time, boring into her and sending her nerve endings into overdrive. His hands manipulated her nipples until every movement shot streaks of pure desire into her womb. She tried to wriggle her hips, pumping with her knees to push him further inside her, but his grip on her was solid as well as gentle. He would not complete the act until she gave him her answer.

"Take me," she begged.

"Are you mine?" Safan repeated in a voice ragged with desire. Maurra felt his muscles tense. His body trembled with unreleased passion. It was clear he was burning as hot as she was.

"Yes."

"It will not be an easy life. My kind will never accept you."

"I know, but I don't care."

"Then say so, Maurra."

"I am yours, Safan."

There was a pause when she heard him give a huge sigh. "As I take you, Maurra," he repeated. In the next instant, he threw back his head and roared. The sound of it vibrated all the way to her bones. At the same time, he rammed himself all the way into her. Her scream caught in the center of her throat. It wasn't until he started pounding away, forcing her to take his whole length with every piercing lunge that she managed to gasp, allowing herself to breathe again.

Her entire focus centered on their connection. On the pain and pleasure flooding her body. On the searing, wonderful agony tearing through her as the bulbous head of his erection bruised her and his cock threatened to tear her apart. His hands were holding her so tightly, she knew she would be sore for days, inside and out. Her breasts swayed painfully as he rocked her forward and back, slamming her against him as he thrust his hips forward. It was all she could do to keep her ass up in the air.

Then, suddenly, he stopped. Before she could comprehend his next step, Safan withdrew from her. Releasing her breasts, he bent her over until her forehead touched the bed, and sank his teeth into her back, bracketing her spine in parallel rows with his jaws, beginning behind her head. Maurra cried out as he slowly dragged his extended eyeteeth over and through her flesh, not stopping until he reached her tailbone. Although the furrows weren't deep, they bled, and to her shock she felt him lapping up her blood. As he tongued her torn skin, Maurra felt a numbing sensation replace the pain, and realized it had to come from his tongue. Something in the Ellinod's saliva was drawing away the sharp agony brought about by his marking her in this manner.

Once he reached her neck again, he lowered his body over hers and placed his hands beneath her and between her legs. "Now we can complete each other," he murmured.

She felt his erection began to re-enter her from the rear the same time his fingers spread her lower lips. She barely had a chance to readjust herself when they covered her clit and started manipulating it. Simultaneously, he lifted his hips, working himself in and out, sliding with greater and greater ease as her body accepted this gentler lovemaking. Coating his heavy length with her juices. Slowly pressing deeper and deeper a bit at a time until he could go no further.

Maurra tried to breathe, but all the air she could manage was ragged, and only halfway filled her lungs. Once again she felt as though she was being impaled, but it was the most wonderful feeling in the world. Every time she inhaled, her body tried to suck his erection further inside her burning channel. But he had gone as far as he could. The slightest movement told her the head of his erection butted against the entrance to her womb.

There was no need to ask what was next. His fingers on her stiff little nub were doing their dance on top of it, as well as lightly running his nails along her silken inner flesh. The fire expanded, rising and ascending inside her with increasing intensity as he masturbated her, as he filled her, and as he brought her closer and closer to perfection.

Just when she thought she was on the verge of combustion, Safan started to pump her with long, relentless strokes. Reality exploded. Intense pleasure flooded every nerve ending. Maurra gasped, unable to fill her lungs with enough air to scream. He closed his fingers around her thighs and continued to hammer into her, grunting with every heavy thrust as he reached for his own pinnacle.

She had no memory of blacking out when the Ellinod's triumphant roar filled the spaceship.

Chapter Thirty-Four
Claimed

"So you were an Orgoran. That explains a lot of things," Maurra lazily commented. She lifted the immense hand from where it was cupping her breast and held it closer to her face.

"How so?" Safan rumbled as he watched her place her palm against his and compare their sizes, as well as their differences. When matched wrist to wrist, her fingertips barely reached his first finger joints.

"Why you weren't dressed like Ellinods I've seen in the past," she explained. "Why you know a smattering of other languages. Why you were in that bar on Cura-Cura. Why you're even built a little differently. Good heavens, Safan! I bet you could wrap the fingers of one hand all the way around my neck!"

"Want me to try?" he half-teased. Turning onto his side so that he faced her, Safan gently drew his fingers around her throat and neck, until his middle finger and thumb met. "You're right. I can." He snorted softly and resumed his position, rolling onto his back next to her, until they were once again touching side to side, skin to skin. He shifted slightly, trying to find a comfortable position again, and Maurra remembered his injuries.

"I need to re-doctor those wounds."

The Ellinod said something that was more of a rumble than a word. Maurra turned to her side to face him. At the same time, she lifted her leg and threw it over his until her knee nudged his testicles. "What was that?"

He cast a light-green gaze at her. "Nothing."

"Naw. You made a comment. I just didn't catch it."

The ridges over his eyes lowered slightly. "Which reminds me, what are you using for a translator?"

She held up her arm so he could see the inner wrist. "The little gizmo your hospital put in me." They could both see it, no more than a pale little disk just under the skin.

"That wasn't meant to be permanent," Safan said.

Maurra shrugged. "It works fine for me, so until it goes bad and I need a new one—"

"Which may be sooner than you think. We need to get you a decent translator if we're..." He paused and turned his face away, but Maurra wasn't about to let it go.

"Aaaand? If we're what?"

He did it again, giving her an indistinguishable grunt in lieu of language. But he had brought it up, and they would have to face the issue sooner or later. Licking her dry lips, Maurra gave his sacs another gentle jiggle.

"Here we are, Safan. Now what? Where do we go from here?"

"What do you mean? I thought we were heading for Vias Daruggah."

By this time, she knew how intelligent the Ellinod was. She could also tell when the creature was figuratively pulling her leg. She started to retort when he suddenly rolled on top of her, supporting his weight on his enormous, muscled arms so as not to crush her. To further surprise her, he started nuzzling her under her chin and over her breastbone. It was a tender gesture, the way he gently ran his mouth over her skin. Nuzzling. Yeah, that was the word. Nuzzling, like a baby searching for his mother's nipple. Without thinking about it, she reached up and took a horn in each hand, and began stroking them, pumping them up and down like she would if they were separate erections. He didn't last long, and with a hard shake of his head, dislodged her hands. Maurra stared up at his unreadable face. She had the urge to scan him, to see what kind of vibes he was putting out, but she hesitated, and that pause surprised herself.

She had changed. The admission wasn't a new one. She knew she had crossed a threshold back on board the Kronner ship. Breached an invisible personal barrier when she trusted him to protect her. She wanted him to trust her in the same way.

From that incident, she had almost foreseen how different it would be, while also knowing they would escape. Oh, yeah, she'd known they would escape. At no point did she feel defeated. Not with Safan behind her, watching her back, protecting her rear. *How* they would get away—now *that* had been the ten-million-credit question. But she had been dead certain it would happen. As certain as she had been about predicting each condemnation and every dismissal thrown at her once she returned to home base.

Yet the black and dismal outcome hadn't fazed her. Not really. In the interim between their escape from the Kronners, to the time she rescued Safan from the mines, Maurra felt as if she was floating in an in-between state, caught between the past and the future, drifting in the present until his lifestream and hers were finally able to reconnect. And when they did, then their universe would go back to the way things were meant to be. Back to the natural order of things.

With her belonging to him.

"You possessed me," she whispered. "You marked me. You claimed me. That means we're inseparable now, doesn't it? You've made me your mate."

His gaze shifted to a spot next to her ear. "It is the way of the Ellinod."

"It is not the way of the Ellinod to claim a mate outside of your species," she contradicted.

The goad worked. Safan gave her an almost angry glare. "My own species has disowned me. To them, I am dead. Therefore I no longer have to follow their edicts. I can take whomever I wish."

Maurra didn't try to hide her smile. "So you chose me."

"No."

"No?"

"*You* chose *me*," he said.

His earnestness got a giggle from her. "All right. Explain that one to me."

"You were rid of me, but you made the choice to come for me at the mines. You led me to your bed. When I reached for you, I gave you the chance to decline."

"And I didn't decline," she concluded.

"No. You didn't."

"I guess changing my mind is out of the question, too?"

His eyes widened, and Maurra sensed a flash of definite worry. She smiled up into his wide-eyed stare to ease his concern. "I'm sorry. I didn't mean it."

"Then why did you say it?" Tension outlined every part of his body. He wasn't convinced. Not yet. Strangely, Maurra felt comforted knowing how deeply she affected him.

"I don't know. Sometimes I'm too fucking flippant. A real smart ass. But know this, Safan." She took his face between her hands and tried to project as much sincerity as possible. "Yes, I came back for you. I'm sorry I didn't do it earlier, but I guess I hadn't figured out what to do with my life, or with my future. I was floating around in some sort of creepy emotional and mental void, waiting for the right moment when something would hit me between the eyes and let me know it was time."

Odd, but at that moment the Ellinod felt more humanistic to her than her own kind. He wasn't conniving. He wasn't vindictive. He was sincere, and his word meant everything to him.

And now she was his mate. He had marked her to keep her with him, and she knew this great brute would protect her until the very last breath in his body.

Maurra felt the tears flooding her eyes. This was love.

When did that revelation come about?

"I'm sorry I teased you," she whispered. "Forgive me."

"Will you tease me again?"

"Oh, yeah. I can't help it. Comes with the package."

He weighed her confession with a slow nod. "You're right. Which is why, for now, I will make the decisions for us."

"What?"

"When we reach Vias Daruggah, we will get you a decent translator."

"We need money to do that, not to mention supplies and fuel. Or did you forget?"

"I did not forget. I have a plan."

"You do? And when were you going to share your plan with me?"

"There's a city called Vi Mot Cu in the southern hemisphere. It has a bar where we might find temporary jobs to pay for more supplies."

Maurra stared at him open-mouthed. "You've been to Vias Daruggah?"

"Not recently," the Ellinod admitted.

"I take it you were there on official business? When you were an Orgoran?"

Safan nodded.

Maurra burst out laughing. "Safan, my dearest mate, why do I get the impression it's going to be a very interesting partnership?"

"Maurra, there is a lot more about me you don't know," the Ellinod promised. "If you think it's interesting now, just wait."

She started to retort, but he bent his face over her breasts again and began to do some wonderfully decadent things to them with his mouth, throwing what she had planned to say out the escape hatch.

It would be a while before they would feel like talking again, but that was all right with her. They had three days to prepare.

Chapter Thirty-Five
Search

Vi Mot Cu was no different from a hundred other space port cities scattered around the galaxy. The rich and elite had their towering abodes clustered in the center of the metropolis, and the grittier, poorer sections lay on the outer fringes.

"What makes this place so special?" Maurra asked as they casually strolled down one avenue, heading for a particular bar where Safan said he had contacts. It was late afternoon, and shop keepers were offering last-minute deals to passers-by before they closed up their stalls for the day. She eyed a vest displayed at one kiosk. It would have been nice to be able to get it. If she was still a JoJo, buying it wouldn't have been a problem. In fact, in a lot of cases, if she had been in uniform, she might have been offered it for free. It was a perk JoJos often came across. And although the administration frowned on such transactions, they were usually overlooked.

Maurra glanced over at the Ellinod, who had stopped momentarily to ask for directions. Despite his attire, Safan projected an air of power and authority, as well as towering over the local inhabitants. Remembering the trouble they'd had trying to get the ship to manufacture a suitable outfit for him, she grinned to herself. Although the previous owners had been much taller, they'd been thinly built. Safan had the height, but he was also as wide as a wall.

"It keeps giving me an error message," he growled. His frustration with the computer was growing. Fearing he might punch out the data board, Maurra pushed him aside to try for herself.

"Are you sure you entered your measurements correctly?" she asked.

"Four times."

After double-checking his input, she pressed ENTER. There was a moment of silence, followed by a click, and a message popped up on the display.

"Data does not compute. Do you want a blanket?"

Maurra laughed so hard, she had tears in her eyes.

Inevitably, they had been forced to recalibrate the onboard computer to accept his data. The results were a tunic and pants that reasonably fit, but they weren't fancy. Neither was Maurra's outfit, but it was for the better. They wanted to present themselves as tough, hard-working but relatively inexpensive merchant shippers, available to haul any kind of cargo as long as it was borderline legit.

The name of the bar was in a language she couldn't translate, but it didn't matter. A bar was a bar was a bar. The interior was dim, crowded, and it stank. Not surprising. Many alien species emitted odors that would clog a ship's vents.

Safan led her over to an empty table that wasn't too far from the center serving area, yet allowed them some amount of privacy. Plus the wall was to their backs. Always a safe move, in her opinion.

She kept one eye on her partner and mate, with the other on the patrons, and a smile lifted one corner of her mouth. She wasn't accustomed to subterfuge. Her status in the past as a JoJo, and the well-recognized uniform she wore, precluded her from trying to slink in and out of places undiscovered. However, it was becoming clearer that Safan was very adept at going undercover and assuming whatever role was needed to catch whatever dirty deeds he'd been assigned to stop. Either it was a skill he excelled in, or he had experienced many opportunities to perfect it.

Propping her boots up on the table, she leaned back in the booth as he ordered for them both. She immediately grabbed his heavily-muscled arm and stared at him.

"Whoa. What are you doing?"

"Ordering us drinks."

"And how do you plan to pay for them?" she almost hissed.

"I have a cred or two to spare," Safan said enigmatically, slapping his hand across the inset tablet flashing their bill. After a moment, their drinks appeared almost instantly through the depression in the center of the tiny table.

Maurra narrowed her eyes. "All right. Tell me what's going on," she asked him directly.

"Do you trust me?"

She answered without having to think about it. "Explicitly."

"Good. Then hear me out. We have a ship for hire, no questions asked about the cargo. At the moment we can't be picky. Got that?" He turned and gave her a stern look. "We get a small percentage up front, enough to cover our immediate expenses and fuel. After we get you a decent translator, we'll take on the cargo, make our delivery, and collect the rest of our fee."

"We're actually going to go through with the job?" she asked over her mug of barritzo. The stuff was mild, compared to the derivatives usually served. She could drink it all day and not get buzzed, which was why she'd ordered it. She couldn't take the chance on being high. Not now. On the other hand, if they really were merchant shippers, it would have been different. She could allow herself to get as soused as she wanted, and know Safan would safely carry her back to the ship.

Taking another sip, she gave her partner another once-over. Despite his attire, if anyone looked like they belonged in law enforcement, Safan did. She made a mental note to ask him how he got into the job, since having a rare and unique talent was part of the criteria, the same way it had been for her.

Safan lowered his mug of quontus and belched. "We are," he answered. "It'll put a few creds in our pockets, and a decent recommendation on our resume if we ever need to dip into these waters again. Speaking of dipping, did you know there's an interstellar bank not five blocks away? We're less than two parsecs away from Kronnaria. What do you think the chances are Vol Brod is using this location to house some of his ill-gotten gains?"

Maurra blinked. "There's an interstellar bank on *this* world?"

"Yeah." He threw a thumb to their left. "That way, if I remember correctly. Go see if you can find out anything. I'll stay here and try to earn us a few credits."

"And try to stay out of trouble while you're at it," she teased. This time he gave her an answering look that told her he had caught the joke. Grinning, she took two more huge gulps of her drink before leaving the bar.

The streets were not as crowded as they had been, which allowed her to jog her way to the bank with ease. Normally interstellar mercantiles remained open around the clock, given the time differences all over the solar system. But sometimes they would "close" for short intervals for small, routine maintenance sweeps. Depending on the planet, those intervals could last for several hours. If she was lucky, she wouldn't encounter such a problem. Maurra didn't know how long they would be on Vias Daruggah, which meant she had to keep the mission tight.

There were several platforms open inside. She claimed one and positioned her face in front of the scanner.

"State your name."

"Maurra Vinish-Nahood." Wincing, she realized she hadn't used her real last name in over two decades. Once she became a JoJo, there was no need for that kind of identification. She had briefly considered using the name she'd used on Alintarus, but because it was an alias, the computers wouldn't recognize her.

"Confirmed. Select your request." Several lines of that indecipherable language popped up on the screen.

"Please translate into InterGalac."

The lines instantly switched to where she could read them. "Requesting status of funds."

"Account number."

"No account number. Requesting availability of funds for client Tramer Vol Brod."

"Request denied without account number."

Uttering a little growl of irritation, Maurra tried a different approach. "Requesting last contact with client Tramer Vol Brod."

"Request denied."

"Fuck!" She'd forgotten how rigidly the bank would protect the identity of its clients. That's why interstellars were as popular as they were. *Is it possible to outwit a bank brain?*

"Requesting transfer of funds."

"Account number of recipient."

That one was easy. Maurra punched in the series of symbols with the ease of long practice. There had been hundreds of times when she had needed a few extra creds while on assignment.

"Account confirmed. Account number of depositor."

"Tramer Vol Brod."

"Account number of depositor," the bank repeated.

"Account number unknown."

"Transfer declined."

Maurra angrily slapped the monitor. Her reflection stared back at her, including the small reddish orb forming in front of her forehead. *Too bad psychic abilities have no effect on computers.*

Maybe not, but they work great on living beings.

Maurra glanced over her shoulder at the creatures coming and going from the bank's other platforms. *Maurra, maybe you're asking the wrong...computer.*

Normally, it was against regulations to invade a person's mind and probe their emotions without that person's knowledge. Whether they agreed to it or not was moot, just as long as they knew she was going to do it. Maurra smiled. The more she thought about it, the more she found herself enjoying the lack of restraints her job had placed on her.

All she needed to do was a full surface scan, hitting every inhabitant within her range. It would be no more than a light skim, just to see if anyone had had any kind of recent contact with her target. It wasn't quite mind-reading, but it was as close to it as she could come.

Tramer Vol Brod. She placed the man's name to the forefront and took several deep breaths to prepare herself.

Tramer Vol Brod.

The platform would give her the privacy she needed. Otherwise, if people saw the ball of psychic energy hovering in front of her face, they might react with fear or disdain.

Tramer Vol Brod.

She had nothing to go on but a hunch. But if someone here knew or had heard of Tramer Vol Brod, it would be enough. Everyone a person came in contact with always left an emotional fingerprint. If he had been here and met someone, she would find the residue, and she would be able to follow that slender clue. All she needed was the spark.

Tramer Vol Brod.

Closing her eyes, Maurra opened her hands and held them palm-out. Her focus strengthened, fueled by the anger she had been nursing ever since the man had kidnapped her.

Taking a deep breath, she sent her blanket of energy out across the city without fear of having it recognized. In its dispersed form it was nearly invisible. No more than the palest luminescence on this world bathing in the rays of a dwarf blue sun.

Tramer Vol Brod.

She passed over people. Through people. Around people. Barely touching their minds as she checked them out. She didn't need to go deep. If her target had been here, either in person or by inter-stellar communications, the memories would be fresh and laying right at the surface.

She touched Safan's mind, but withdrew without brushing through it. She could sense her image already resting on the surface, and beneath it simmered his emotions brought about by memories of last night. She got the faintest whisper of him interacting with another person. Maybe a client. Even so, the Ellinod was slightly pissed about having his original train of thought interrupted. Smiling, Maurra went on.

Tramer Vol Brod.

There was less traffic on the roadways and in the skies as people settled down for the evening. Maurra wondered how Safan was doing as she whirled through large groups and pockets of sentient creatures. She knew without asking that he was as eager to make Vol Brod pay for what had been done to them as she was.

Tramer Vol Brod.

A visage suddenly flashed into her mind with blinding clarity. Maurra could see the tall, thin man with intense gray eyes as if he were standing before her. The expression on his face was a mixture of impatience and worry.

She instantly grasped the mind of the person holding the information she needed with psychic hands and slid invisible fingers further into his brain.

Vol Brod had been here. He had been here...yesterday. To withdraw his money. To take what he had deposited before moving on. His presence had left behind a nauseous reaction.

Maurra whirled around with her breath caught in her throat. He had been here on this world yesterday, and she finally had a clue as to where he might be.

She ran back to the bar to get Safan.

Chapter Thirty-Six
Bounty

Maurra turned down the street where the bar was located, and saw Safan emerge from the establishment. He was talking with a creature of a species she wasn't familiar with, but from the Ellinod's gestures and expressions, she guessed they had landed a job. He looked up as she joined them.

"Maurra, this is..." The name he pronounced wasn't pronounceable for her. Neither could her translator find any equivalent. She gave the creature a slight nod to acknowledge him and remained quiet to listen, but her senses were revving, sending her warning signals of something imminent. Something dangerous. Telling her not to trust the large slug-like alien. She was tempted to scan it when Safan continued.

"We're taking on a load of ansia byrite crystals and taking it to Trisom Villig."

Maurra bobbed her head again and dismissed the client. Ansia byrite required a special containment field to haul, and their ship had that equipment. If Safan believed dealing with this alien was safe enough, she had to learn to trust his instincts as well. She continued to play mute.

The creature squidged out a few more syllables of its impossible language, to which Safan answered in his deep voice. The comparison would have been laughable if it hadn't been so serious. Adding another watery blurp, the thing gave a nod in reply and slithered off on its monopod underbelly, to her great relief. Unfortunately the warning signals didn't lessen with the thing's departure. She debated whether to say something. Again, she was interrupted when Safan placed a hand on her back and turned to head for their ship.

"Let's go."

"Safan, something about that client isn't right," she finally managed to say.

"The client isn't the most law-abiding of creatures. Of course you're going to get bad vibes from it."

"No, I think it's more than that."

He shot her a questioning look. "All right. I'll heed the warning and keep up my guard. Anything else?"

"Yes! I got a lead on Vol Brod!"

"Hush. I know. So did I," he answered mysteriously.

"What? Why? How?"

"In the ship, Maurra. There's too many invisible ears out here, and too many eyes watching our every move. Don't forget we're strangers out here, and everyone is watching to see if we can be trusted, not to mention our identities."

Identities? She bit her lip and remained silent until they were back inside the *Lorrmandi II.* As the door sealed shut, she followed the Ellinod into the bridge area.

"All right. Spill it." She watched as he punched in the coordinates for Trisom Villig before looking back at her. Something was bothering him. Had been bothering him ever since she rejoined him at the bar. At the time she had dismissed it as being a result of their job offer, but not anymore. By now it was pouring off of him in waves.

"Vol Brod has a bounty on our heads," he told her.

"He *what?*"

"Somehow he's found out I've escaped the mines, and you and I have hooked back up. The man is smart as well as dangerous. He knows us pairing up has to mean we're coming after him."

Maurra took a step back. "How did you find out?"

"The mine incident was broadcast over the news service in the bar. It mentioned my escape and the resulting bounty. Fortunately, my escape is only a priority two alert, since I'm not considered a danger. But everyone is being told to be on the watch for an Ellinod in the company of a red-haired human. The only thing that wasn't mentioned was your psi powers, or that you used to be a JoJo."

"That's to our advantage. But because I helped you escape, that makes both of us wanted criminals. Safan, is someone going to come after you to take you back to the mines?" She cursed herself for not thinking about it earlier. Another thought struck her. She had told the warden she was heading for Farak Took Mees. That planetary system was in the opposite direction from Bansheer Prime. Safan's choice had inadvertently given them a few days' grace. To her relief, the Ellinod shook his massive head.

"No. They won't come after me, but that doesn't mean Vol Brod hasn't hired a bounty hunter or two to search for us. Maurra, the reward is ten million creds."

"Oh, sweet heavens!" She took another step back and stumbled. She would have fallen onto the floor in shock if Safan hadn't grabbed her first and pulled her against his massive chest. She clutched his shirt with white knuckles and pressed her cheek against it as his warmth seeped into her.

Ten million creds? The number was simply too large for her to comprehend. Where did the man get that kind of money? Just how much had the man charged his customers to watch her and Safan screw? For that matter, how many customers subscribed?

"What are we going to do?" she murmured more to herself than to her partner. Strange, how being held like this was managing to calm her. Allowing her to gather her wits back around her so she could think more clearly.

"Right now? We refuel, grab our cargo, and deliver it. You'll have to wait a bit longer to replace that translator. Sorry."

"That's all fine and good for now, but what about afterwards? What's to stop someone else from putting a bounty out on us?"

Drawing her away, he lowered his face closer to hers as he continued to grip her by the arms. "Unless by some sort of miracle I'm given a reprieve, it's a possibility we'll have to face. You knew you would be guilty of collusion when you came to rescue me, didn't you?"

Yeah. She had known it, but the need to rescue him from the mines had been more important to her than the risk of being branded a criminal. Maurra gave a nervous laugh. "I'm not used to being on this side of the law."

"Neither am I. Guess that makes it a learning process for both of us."

Safan released her and ordered the ship to head for the nearest fueling station, then reached into his pants pocket to hand her a receiving disk. "Here's our advance. There's four hundred creds on it. We get another four when the recipient acknowledges the delivery. Can you re-supply while I have the engines scanned?"

"Yeah. Sure. Anything in particular you want, or that I need to know?"

"I'll eat anything except gorse. I'm allergic to it."

Maurra paused and gave him a small smile. "Funny. So am I. All right. I'll be as quick as possible. Where are we picking up the job?"

"We're meeting the Xelopian over on pad six-two-five," Safan told her. "If you're not back here in forty quadrills, I'll meet you over there."

Maurra quickly converted the time into units she could follow and set her internal clock. "Let me have that little cylindrical communications device again, just in case."

Safan found the tiny capsule where she'd left it on the console and handed it to her. As their fingers touched, she was surprised when his hand grasped hers. Maurra looked up to see a worried frown on his face.

"Watch your back, Maurra," he said, his gravelly voice filled with concern. "I don't completely trust the Xelopian, but we had no other choice. Until we get our bearings, every transaction is risky at this point."

She nodded and turned to leave, but his grip remained firm. She was about to ask if there was anything else but she was silenced with a kiss. It was a long, warm one that sent little shivers all the way to her toes. Other than his hand and his lips, the Ellinod didn't touch her. There was no other bodily contact, but she felt as if she was being lovingly embraced. More and more, the Ellinod was managing to find ways to bind her to him. Not just physically, but mentally and emotionally.

When the kiss was over, she quickly left the ship and headed back into town.

Chapter Thirty-Seven
Ploy

Everyone is being told to be on the watch for an Ellinod in the company of a red-haired human.

Maurra stared at the long strands she held in her hand. Normally she wore her hair in a braid, or bound with max bands. The color never mattered to her, but it mattered now. The first thing people tended to notice was a person's species. The second was color — the color of their hide, their clothing...or their fur.

Screw it. If changing her hair color meant the difference between being identified or being overlooked, she would change it, since there was little Safan could do to change his appearance. "Short of cutting off his horns," she muttered. "And there's no way I'd let that happen." Considering how his horns directly affected his sex drive, removing them could be as disastrous as having him castrated.

She knew most of the smaller markets in town were already closed for the evening, but there was always one place on every planet with a space port where ship crews could go to restock. Normally it would be located near the port for convenience, so she headed for the rear of the port's main building.

The market was open, as she'd expected, and thankfully customers were sparse. Grabbing a hover sled, she began accumulating a nice mountain of items. There was no reason to worry about using up all the creds on the card. For one thing, the ship wouldn't be able to hold four hundred creds' worth of supplies. For another, she had to remember Safan had yet to pay for the ship's fuel.

Satisfied she had all the rations they'd need, she headed over to where the personal hygiene items were displayed. Most of the things there were either foreign or unrecognizable to her. All except for the dye. She grabbed the first color that looked appealing and tossed it onto the sled. It was getting close to the time when Safan said if she wasn't back, she could meet him where they were to pick up their cargo.

Guiding the sled up to the check-out terminal, she waited for the scanners to tally up the cost, then stuck the card into the payment slot.

"Will that be all?" a metallic-sounding voice inquired.

"Yeah."

"Can I help you with anything else?"

"Yeah. Can I get directions to pad six-two-five?"

A flat image popped up onto the screen with the path from the market to the site highlighted. Maurra grimaced. It would be her luck that six-two-five was at the farthest end of the landing field. At least she had the sled to transport her purchase.

The scanner spat her card back to her, and the gates opened to let her out. Maurra headed straight for the landing area where Safan said he would meet her.

Vias Daruggah had no moon, but the panorama of stars overhead more than made up for the lack, in her opinion. Of course, the occasional street light flooded all but the brightest stars. Still, Maurra kept glancing up at the swirl of color. A nearby nebula washed pinks and reds and purples near the horizon, giving the impression of a faux sunset. She had no idea how long the days were on this planet, but it didn't matter. As soon as they had their fuel, supplies, and cargo loaded, they were taking off. The sooner they finished the job, the sooner they could get back to tracking Vol Brod.

As she approached the pads, she noticed the port was nearly deserted. She paused in her musing and frowned. *What gives?* Normally space ports were the busiest areas on a planet. *Must be their slow time of night.*

In the distance she could see the *Lorrmandi II*. On the pad next to it was a round, nearly spherical ship. There was no activity on the ground. Neither could she see anything going on through the ship's main viewscreen. *Maybe they've already got everything loaded.*

Reaching underneath her breast, Maurra touched the communications link through her blouse with her thumb. "Lorri, this is your captain."

"Yes, Captain?"

"Has cargo been loaded?"

"There has been no cargo loaded," the ship crisply responded.

Maurra came to an abrupt halt. The hover sled gently bumped into the back of her thighs. Instinctively, she sent out a mental search for Safan, and the image that came back to her turned her blood into ice water.

There was nothing. No sense of him, no emotional reply.

Absolutely zilch.

"Lorri, is the Ellinod aboard?"

"Negative."

"Is the Ellinod nearby?"

"Undeterminable," the ship said.

Of course the ship wouldn't know where he is if he isn't wearing a link. She had forgotten she had be specific with her phrasing.

"Lorri, scan for life forms. Locate the Ellinod."

"Ellinod located."

"Where is the Ellinod?"

"The Ellinod is two hundred forty-eight point two meters from the ship."

Two hundred and... "How far away is the Ellinod from me?"

"The Ellinod is one hundred ninety point eight meters from your location."

Maurra turned around and scanned the area. Other than the main building...

"Lorri, how far away am I from the port's main offices?"

"You are one hundred eighty-eight point one meters from the port's main offices."

Why would Safan be at the main building and not with the ship?

He went to pay for gas. No. I've got the card. Is he waiting for me to join him and give him the card? But then he would have told me to meet him at the offices.

Or maybe there was some unfinished business he needed to tend to over there.

Or maybe the slug client needed him there.

Or maybe...

Fuck this. It was too quiet and too deserted. Something was wrong. She knew it as clearly as if it was a sign flashing in front of her.

Maurra felt her powers coming to the fore. Raising her hands over her head, she went in search of the Ellinod, sending out a wide wave of psionic energy across the platforms and through the long, squatty building sitting at the edge of the landing field. She found him almost immediately, but again something wasn't right. There was no reaction to her gentle probe. No response at all. It was almost as if...

"He doesn't want me to come after him."

Why?

"Because something or someone is waiting for me to join him."

Widening her search, she opened up to receive any other signals, and found them immediately. There were six others in the same vicinity as Safan—three unrecognizable aliens, two that felt vaguely like Triconians, and one humanoid.

No. She stiffened. *One human.*

In one enormous flash of comprehension, Maurra realized she and Safan had been duped. The slug client had been a ploy, setting them up. Leading them right into a trap.

And there was only one answer as to who was behind this whole elaborate set-up. She knew who the one human was.

"Very well, Vol Brod," Maurra murmured with rising anger. "I'll take your bet, and I raise you two lives. Now I call. Show me what you've got. Show me your hand, you conniving, suckface snot worm, because you have no idea who or what you're dealing with."

She began walking toward the port offices, her hands gripped into fists by her sides. The crimson ball of energy bathed her forehead in light, and made her surroundings glow as she quickly strode across the landing pads.

This time, there was no implant in her back to prevent her from enacting the full force of her abilities. If Tramer Vol Brod thought he had the upper hand, he was going to find out he was sorely mistaken.

And if he had harmed Safan in any way...

Chapter Thirty-Eight
Devious

Every cell in her body was on high alert. Every particle of her power was coiled, ready to spring, ready to strike, ready to be released. Maurra could feel her energy growing as she neared the building. But with the feel of her psion strength heating her blood, she also knew she was walking into a potentially explosive situation. Vol Brod would know she wasn't constrained. Therefore he must have some sort of plan to keep her reined in.

Keep a calm and level head, girl. Be a JoJo again. No emotions, just reason. No sudden moves, just stay calm and in control. And certainly no barging in to throw your weight around. Shield yourself and take in the situation first before you act.

Maurra had faced similar situations in the past. Hell, in nearly every instance where she had gone after a criminal, they had thought they had the "perfect way" to stop her. Practically every known weapon in the universe, and some that had just been invented, had been used against her. Only by keeping her wits about her had she survived the attacks.

Except this time would be different. This time Safan's life may be at risk.

Hell, nothing! You know it's at risk! What else could Vol Brod use against me?

That was why she'd sense a human figure with him. That was why Safan was keeping himself closed off from her — to protect her. Except the one thing he couldn't do was shelter his body's reactions from her. That's how she knew he was in danger. Otherwise she would be getting a feeling of contentment, or hunger, or worry from him. Some emotion, any emotion. But to get such a blank void was as telling as any message letting her know the truth.

Or maybe he knows that. Maybe he knows that by shutting himself away, he's sending me a signal of some sort?

If they survived this — no. Wait. *After* they survived this meeting, they would sit down and formulate a specific code, so that if something like this should happen to them again in the future...

Maurra mentally paused as the impact of her admission settled inside her. Her future was his now. Together. The both of them were as one entity from now on. She knew it as much as he did. They had become inseparable, bound together not just because of the sex or the trauma of the kidnapping, but because something deeper and stronger had been forged. It was an emotion she had never felt with another being, human or otherwise, but it was there. And if she dug deep enough, she knew she would find it inside Safan, too. That was why he had marked her. Even without admitting their feelings to each other, they still understood each other perfectly.

As she approached the building, she could see most of the inside lights were out. That meant the people who were manning the port were probably being held hostage inside, along with Safan. Otherwise the place would be lit up brighter than daytime.

Like most space ports she was familiar with, the long, low building was built partially sunk into the ground to protect it from crashes and the occasional engine backwash. There were no real windows, other than the narrow wall slits used for confirming a visual ID. The single reinforced turret on top of the building was the main control tower.

A sudden thought made her call back to the ship. "Lorri, have you been refueled?"

"Affirmative, Captain."

Thank the heavens for that. That may explain why Safan had gone to the offices in the first place.

Pausing outside the doors, Maurra glanced over her shoulder at the *Lorrmandi II* and the ship parked next to it. She had mistakenly assumed the spheroid was their client's craft. Common sense now told her it had to be either Vol Brod's, or it belonged to the creatures he had hired to go after her and the Ellinod.

You have one major advantage going for you, girl. They don't know you're already aware of them. That's your element of surprise. Go in as if nothing's wrong.

Go in...clear.

Closing her eyes, Maurra took several deep breaths. She could feel her orb dissolving, diminishing until it was absorbed back into her mind. But it remained at ready, less than a heartbeat away from taking in everything and everyone around her.

Two one-hundredths of a second. I need less than two one-hundredths of a second.

She pasted a look of impatience across her face and hit the switch on the outer blast doors. They slid open with a hiss, revealing the secondary doors. She slapped the next switch to open them, revealing a building sitting in pitch black.

"Hey! What's the matter? Having a power outage?" she yelled into the darkness. "Helloooo! Safan! Are you in here? I got the card if you need to pay for the fuel!"

All was silent. Another bad sign. Not to mention she was receiving some seriously bad vibes. Bad enough to taste like bile on her tongue.

Still acting confused and pissed, Maurra added, "Where's the fucking light console in this place?"

As if on cue, a single beam of light appeared in one of the doorways leading to another part of the building. Maurra obediently followed it.

"Hellooo! Anybody here? Who's supposed to be on duty tonight? Hey! Your lights aren't working!"

The beam was enigmatic. A weaving little ball that flittered and fluttered like a luminescent bubble through one door, through a room, and through another door. Its golden yellow glow seemed innocuous in a place like this.

Maurra continued to follow it from one dark area to another, while realizing it was leading her into the farthest part of the building. She was drawing nearer to where she knew Safan was located, along with the other life forms. She also knew the ball of light was keeping her eyes unaccustomed to the blackness, the same way she knew it was turning her into a perfect target.

Her instincts saved her.

As soon as she turned the corner into one of the rooms, her mind reacted, and before she could think, her psion shield encased her in pure mental energy as several guns went off simultaneously. The force of their rays sprayed over and around her, without affecting her. When the attackers finally got the drift that their trap had failed, the lights suddenly came back on, and through the glare Maurra found herself glowering at the very man who had caused her so much grief. But it wasn't the sight of Tramer Vol Brod that made her gasp in shock. It was seeing Safan standing helplessly behind him, unable to move because he was encased in a highly-charged cocoon that glittered as it slowly rotated around him. A pretty but wholly deadly Volpter's Cage.

However, it was clear that the Ellinod hadn't been very cooperative about getting inside it. Along the far wall lay at least half a dozen creatures, all with broken limbs, and all of them leaking bodily fluids. At least two of them appeared to be dead.

Vol Brod chuckled, drawing her attention back to him. "Another point for your side, JoJo. Oh, excuse me. I meant ex-JoJo. But even stripped of your designation, you're a powerful enemy. Powerful and deadly. Speaking of stripped..." His eyes roamed over her body and her simple clothing. "That outfit does nothing for you. I much prefer to see you naked."

Maurra clenched her jaw but remained silent. Vol Brod loved to boast almost as much as he loved to taunt. She was willing to see how far this drama would play out. Until then, she had to find the switch to the Volpter's Cage.

She glanced over at the three creatures still standing with their pulsar rifles in their multiple arms. Ferni Ceserrites. A sentient albeit relatively stupid life form. Vol Brod had found another money-hungry species to do his dirty bidding. Not present were the two alien entities she'd sensed earlier. Apparently they were the missing port employees. The fact that she had been able to locate them told her they were still alive.

She looked back at Safan. "Are you all right?"

"Yes." His voice was strained. He was fighting to remain absolutely still, but she could already see blood saturating his torn clothes and running down his arms where the lethal crystalline razors had sliced him.

"He's fine for now, but that doesn't mean he'll remain that way," Vol Brod sneered. He finally produced his left hand from where he had been keeping it behind his back. A little crystal sliver sat firmly grasped in his palm. The trigger. The detonator. "Are you familiar with a Volpter's Cage?"

She shook her head, continuing to play the fool. The pale pink glow of her shield made it look as though the whole room was the same color. There was no way she was going to lower the only protection she had against the three Ferni Ceserrites, who were moving around, changing positions, encircling her as they re-aimed their weapons. The earlier blasts had been white in color. That meant the rifles were set to kill. The instant she lowered her shield, they wouldn't hesitate to fire again. Vol Brod wanted her dead.

"I've heard of them."

The man's grin broadened. "See this device in my hand? It controls the cage containing your lover. With a single thought, I can either set him free, or I can command it to implode. Which means he becomes nothing more than a pile of finely-chopped chunks of stew meat."

Maurra crossed her arms over her chest. With her shield emanating from the orb hovering on her forehead, she didn't need to use her hands to keep herself protected.

"Pretty ingenious, graghole." *That's right, Maurra. Continue to compliment the idiot while he's stupidly unaware of the mistake he's made.* "I gotta hand it to you. All this time we thought we were tracking you down, when really you were following us, waiting for the moment you could catch us unawares."

Vol Brod laughed. "You're right. It *was* ingenious of me, wasn't it? Just as it was ingenious for me to think about purchasing this cage from my wonderful dealers over there." He motioned toward the creatures guarding her. "When I heard on the news that the Ellinod had escaped from the mines, and that he had been aided by a red-headed woman, it wasn't hard to figure out what you had in mind. I knew I had to stop you. After all, I don't want to spend the rest of my life having to keep looking over my shoulder. It would make my life miserable."

Gee. We would make his *life miserable? How ironic is that?*

"There's just one thing that I haven't quite figured out, though," Maurra admitted, tilting her head to give him a puzzled stare. "Why *are* you going to all this trouble?"

Vol Brod shared her puzzled look. "To stop you from coming after me. I thought I just made that part very clear."

"True. True." She nodded. "I meant, it's just the three of us involved. What makes you think we're out for revenge? For that matter, how do you think we'd be able to get any sort of revenge on you for what you did to us? After all, no one believes us. It's your word against ours if you're ever caught and brought in for questioning. We don't have any proof you instigated this whole thing. No one knows it was you who had the Kronners kidnap me and the Ellinod, or that you held us captive in the Kronner ship. No one but the three of us know anything about it because you destroyed all the evidence, including the vid equipment, and you made sure to murder all your accomplices when you blew up the Kronner ship."

Vol Brod shrugged. "I had planned on doing that long before I had you two taken. I couldn't afford to have them say anything, no matter how much I paid them."

Maurra sighed loudly. "To think, you went to all that trouble simply because I had you put away?"

To her surprise, Vol Brod chuckled. "Oh, I was highly upset at the time, let me tell you! There I was, at the brink of the most lucrative deal I'd ever made, and you busted me. You testified against me, and I got six years for it on Blancher's Asteroid. *Six years.*" His face suddenly darkened with anger. "I had six years to come up with the perfect scheme to get my revenge. Six years to make up for all the money I'd lost. Thanks to you and your lover, I have more creds now than I'll ever be able to spend, even if I live to be a hundred and fifty!"

"But why me?" Safan gasped. The sharp blades were so close to him, every breath he took meant a bit of skin was filleted from his body. Maurra could see blood puddling under his feet.

Again, Vol Brod gave a bark of laughter. "That was the Kronners' idea. When I approached them with my deal, they begged to include you. It seems you and they had had some run-ins in the past over some illegal cargo, or something like that. They had you pegged the moment you entered that bar on Cura-Cura." He looked at Maurra. "It was pure luck you entered that bar right afterwards."

"So everything you had planned came together that night," Maurra clarified.

"Actually, no. You see, I really had planned on having you fuck a Par Matta, but when I got a good look at the Ellinod's package, I knew I'd found the perfect partner for you."

Maurra placed her hands on her hips. At last, everything was revealed with total clarity. Vol Brod's plan had come together so well. The only element he had changed was exchanging Safan for the Par Matta. She closed her eyes, refusing to think how this nightmare could have been different if Safan hadn't been selected.

"All right. So I'm guessing your plan now is to dispatch me and Safan as quickly as possible so you can get back to spending your unholy amount of money you earned selling subscriptions so people could watch us fuck."

"Sorry to be the bearer of bad tidings," Vol Brod said in a condescending tone. "I thought I'd first let you watch the Ellinod get diced into fine mulch. Then, after the rest of my crew get here with their weapons, we would see how long you could hold out before we managed to penetrate that shield of yours."

"Aren't you forgetting something?" Maurra asked. "What if I try to stop you first by freezing your minds?"

Vol Brod threw back his head and laughed heartily. At the same time, he gave a gesture with his free hand, and three beams of white light struck her shield's outer shell.

"Go ahead, psion! Go ahead and try! Everyone knows that psions can't penetrate their own shields. The moment you drop yours to try and stop me, my agents will get you!"

Maurra slowly raised her arms until they were straight out in front of her. Her hands were cupped with the palms facing out. A sword of blood-red light connected her forehead to her fingers. Maurra narrowed her eyes at the man.

"Hey, graghole. Sorry to be the bearer of bad tidings, but that bit about not being able to penetrate a shield? That only applies to the regular JoJos. To the Joramansu. Guess you didn't know I'm a Jurasu Roja, did you? A Jurasu Roja. Do you know what that means, you piece of grot shit?"

Before he could reply, she sent out a burst of concentrated psychic energy. The beam slid through her shield without dispersing the pale aura, and struck Vol Brod squarely in the face. The man's eyes nearly bugged out of his head, and his body dropped like a discarded coat. Maurra turned to look at the three aliens, who suddenly stopped firing and took off running out of the building.

She shut down her shield as the little red orb on her forehead continued to whirl and dance. Walking over to where Vol Brod lay in a paralyzed heap on the floor, she reached out with the toe of her boot and nudged his cheek where it was lying against the floor, lifting his face until his eyes were directed at her.

"It means I was a level red JoJo," she finished telling him. "Top one percent, you worthless piece of snot. Next time, do your homework a little more thoroughly."

Reaching down, she found the control for the Volpter's Cage tightly clutched in his hand.

"Maurra."

She gave the Ellinod a warm smile. "Don't worry. I have total control of him." That being said, she mentally ordered the cage to shut itself down. The shearing blades fell onto the floor and shattered into harmless bits with the sound of tiny bells. Safan swayed in relief. Wordlessly, she strode over and put her arms around the huge beast to keep him from collapsing. The Ellinod reciprocated, holding her tightly against him and pressing his face into her hair. Several moments passed in silence.

"Close call," she finally murmured into his warm chest.

"Yes."

"So what's our next move?"

She felt him sigh. The sound of it in his chest was like an enormous set of bellows. "We could take him back to Ellinod for trial..." His voice tapered off. Maurra leaned back to look up at him.

"What's the penalty for kidnapping an Orgoran?" she asked.

Safan grinned. "Life in the mines."

"Gee. Is everyone who breaks the law penalized with life in the mines?" she halfway jested. "Remind me not to spit on the sidewalk."

"That's a level three," he smiled. "The mines are sentenced only if it's a capital one offense."

"Like screwing someone of the wrong species? That's a capital one offense?"

"It is." He nodded in Vol Brod's direction. "We could take him in, but it would do no good. Our justice system won't condemn unless there's proof. Like you said earlier, it would simply be our word against his."

"What about *his* word against his?" she countered, her smile growing wider by the second.

Safan frowned. "I'm afraid I don't understand."

Reaching underneath her breast, Maurra pulled out the little communications capsule. "Lorri, did you get all that?"

"Yes, Captain," the ship promptly replied.

"Play back first ten seconds for verification, please."

There was a click.

"Another point for your side, JoJo. Oh, excuse me. I meant ex-JoJo. But even stripped of your designation, you're a powerful enemy. Powerful and deadly. Speaking of stripped, that outfit does nothing for you. I much prefer to see you naked."

"Give a point to the man," Safan murmured as he bent over to kiss her. "I have to agree with him on that matter. I certainly prefer you naked."

Chapter Thirty-Nine
Forward

Tramer Vol Brod began screaming for leniency even before the Grand Justice on Ellinod gave him life in the Bansheer mines.

"You can't do that!" the man shrieked. "I'm not Ellinod! You can't sentence me to that place!" He fought the guards who grabbed him by his arms, and struggled as they easily carted him away to a holding cell to await transport. "I protest! I was set up! You can't do this to me! She recorded me without my permission! She illegally froze my mind, and she can't do that because she's not a JoJo anymore! I demand real justice! I *order* you to let me be judged by someone of my own species!"

Maurra smiled and gave a little wave goodbye as Vol Brod disappeared behind the closing doors.

"Safan Bieret Alvvi Diroo."

The Ellinod briskly turned to face the Grand Justice. Maurra remained beside him, despite the fact that her presence was unprecedented. If anyone protested, no one had voiced it.

When they had arrived on Ellinod, they had immediately taken Vol Brod and the incriminating audio to the Grand Orgoran Station. In a few short days, they were ordered to present themselves at the hearing.

The Grand Justice was headed by two elderly Ellinod. Their skin was creased into a thousand folds across their bodies, and their hands trembled, but their voices were firm and their eyes were bright. Age and infirmity did not affect the minds of this species, Maurra noted.

"You have brought to light the truth about your abduction and forced intimacy," one judge intoned. "However, the truth also remains that you consented to have sexual relations with a non-Ellinod female."

Safan nodded but remained silent. Any additional word or gesture he made at this point would be detrimental to his case.

"The initial ruling to strip you of your title of Orgoran stands. Neither will you be able to hold title on any job or acquisition, other than what you are naturally entitled through your family namesake."

Safan nodded again. Maurra cast a sideways glance in his direction. Family namesake? What did that mean?

"In regards to your sentence, sending you to the Bansheer mines, we have taken into account your past history and work record as Orgoran. We have taken into consideration the cost and danger you took on to bring Tramer Vol Brod to justice, in order that he may serve his sentence for the needless deaths of the Kronners. Therefore, it is our decision to reduce your sentence to time served." The Grand Justice muttered something to his co-judge, then turned back to them. "Justice has been served. Justice has spoken. You are free to go."

Maurra stood in stunned silence as the two Ellinod got up from their seats and left the room, along with the small group of spectators who had been watching from the back. Out of the corner of her eye, she saw one Ellinod crinkle his— her?— nose at the sight of the parallel scars running down Maurra's bared back. The outfit had been Safan's request, and Maurra understood why. By showing her scars, she was proving she had accepted him as her mate, and that she was allowed to be with him wherever he went on the planet. Including standing beside him during the final sentencing.

She looked up at Safan and grinned. "That's it? It's over?"

"Yes." He let out a deep sigh of relief. "It's over. I'm no longer an escaped criminal. Come." He placed a hand to her back and began to lead her out of the building.

"Hey, explain something to me. What did that judge mean by family namesake?"

"What?"

"He...or was he a she? Anyway, that judge said you would not be allowed any sort of title except what you were naturally allowed to have through your family namesake. What did he-she mean by that?"

Safan stopped once they were outside and turned to look at her. His large, warm hand continued to rest against her back, and every so often she felt his fingertips gently caress the scars.

"It means I still have my family title and wealth."

She was unaware her jaw had dropped to waist level. "You're *wealth*? Are you telling me you're *wealthy*?"

"It is a pre-requisite for being Orgoran," he stated.

"Are you telling me we were never in danger of starving to death?" Anger sent little flashes of heat into her face when she thought of how worried she had been about their lack of funds. Safan held up his free hand to halt her tirade.

"At the time you rescued me from the mines, and we landed on Vias Daruggah, I had a few meager creds of my own that I'd kept hidden away, but that was all. And that was all I would be allowed to have until I could contact my family again and withdraw more funds."

"There was an international bank on Vias Daruggah."

"True," Safan acknowledged. "But I told you, obtaining funds would have been restricted to me until I contacted my family." He paused to give her a moment to cool down, then added, "I have never lied to you, Maurra."

"But we could have starved to death," she persisted. "We could have run out of fuel in the middle of sp—"

Safan shut her up in the most effective way he knew. He kissed her. A long, slow, toe-tingling kiss that made her smile when he drew back.

"All right. Now that I have your attention, we have a decision to make," he murmured.

"I'm listening," Maurra said. *I'm listening with a creamy wetness rolling down the inside of my thighs because of what your kisses do to me.*

"You do understand that I no longer hold any position of authority."

"Neither do I."

"Which means we need to find some sort of employment to help support ourselves."

"What kind of job would we be good at? Why can't we live off of your family money for the time being? I think we've earned ourselves a little vacation."

Safan gave her a bemused look. "To access any additional funds, I have to be gainfully employed. It's—"

"A pre-requisite?"

He chuckled. "A requirement."

"All right. Any suggestions?"

"I was thinking, because we've both been in law enforcement, and we have the training—"

"And I have the power."

"I thought we would make a great pair of bounty hunters."

Maurra raised an eyebrow. "You're not kidding, are you?"

"I'm very serious," Safan said. "Think about it. Bringing in the bad guys is what we do best. We just won't have to wear a uniform, or abide by the strict rules we had to follow when we wore it. What do you think?"

"I think you may be the brains of this outfit," Maurra admitted with a little giggle. "All right. We're going to be bounty hunters. What do you suggest we do first?"

Giving her another little push, the Ellinod started to lead her in the direction of the space port. "First, we go to the market and get you a decent translator."

"If there's a first, there has to be a second."

"Second, we need to look into getting the ship's toilet lowered. You can't keep using a stepladder every time you need to use it. And third—"

"There's a third?"

"Yes." He stopped and turned her around, and pulled her against his body until he enveloped her in his embrace as he kissed her again. Maurra could feel his thick erection pressing into her belly. She playfully wriggled her hips, and earned herself a breathy groan. It wasn't until his lips nuzzled hers that she was able to speak.

"I'm all for the third. What are we waiting for? In fact, I have a better idea. Let's make number three our number one priority. The rest can wait a while longer."

"I like your suggestion." He released her, but kept one hand on her back as they continued to walk back to the ship.

"Oh, one more thing I've been meaning to ask you," Maurra said. "How did your horn get all twisted like that?"

"I got caught up in a bar fight," Safan admitted. "Off duty."

She looked up at the chagrined expression on his face and burst out laughing. Her feeling of joy remained with her until long after sunset, when exhaustion finally claimed them both.

About the Author

Linda loves to write sweet and sensuous romance with a fantasy, paranormal, or science fiction flair. As the author of over 100 books, her technique is often described as being as visual as a motion picture or graphic novel.

She's a wife, mother, grandmother, and retired Kindergarten and music teacher who lives in a small south Texas town near the Gulf coast, where she delves into other worlds filled with daring exploits, adventure, and intense love.

She's had numerous best sellers, including 10 consecutive #1s. Also included in her achievements, she's been named Author of the Year, and her book *Lord of Thunder* is an Epic Ebook "Eppie" Award Winner for Best Erotic Sci-Fi Romance.

In addition, Linda also writes naughty humorous romances under the name of Carolyn Gregg, horror under the pseudonym of Gail Smith, and elementary teacher workbooks as L. G. Mooney.

For more information about her books, up-coming and new releases, contests, and giveaways, and to sign up for her newsletter, please visit her website:

http://www.LindaMooney.com

Science Fiction Romances by Linda Mooney

The Battle Lord Saga
> The Battle Lord's Lady
> Her Battle Lord's Desire
> A Battle Lord's Heart
> One Battle Lord's Fate
> This Battle Lord's Quest
> Every Battle Lord's Nightmare
> Their Battle Lord's Sacrifice

The D'Jacques Dynasty
> Lucien

Beauty's Alien Beast

The Charm

Deep

A Different Yesterday

The Final Pleasure

Forbitten

Star Girl Series
> The Gifted
> The Gifting

HeartFast Series
> HeartFast
> HeartCrystal
> HeartStorm

His by Right

His Last Request

Knight of Darkness

The Thunder Trilogy
> Lord of Thunder

Passion of Thunder
Wings of Thunder
Mine Until Midnight
My Strength, My Power, My Love
Neverwylde
Rhea 41070
Runner's Moon

Jebaral
Tiron
Simolif
Challa
Yarrolam

UnderSilver
Vall's Will
X-Troller
Zonaton

Made in the USA
Columbia, SC
21 September 2020